"Has anyone ever told you how beautiful you are?"

Dash asked, his gaze sliding like silk across Savannah's face.

No one, not ever. "No."

"Is the rest of the world blind?"

His words were followed by silence. A silence that had spanned years for Savannah. A silence that echoed in the darkest chambers of her soul. No man had whispered sweet nothings to her. No man had looked past her flaw and seen the desirable woman she longed to be. No man but Dash.

His mouth came down on hers, shattering the silence with his hungry need, shattering the self-imposed discipline she'd held herself under all these years. She wrapped herself in his embrace and returned the kiss with the potency of her own need.

Dash moaned and kissed her hard and fast, and she responded with every ounce of her being. She kissed him as if she'd been waiting all her life for this moment, for this man.

D0980425

Dear Reader,

Welcome to Silhouette **Special Edition** . . . welcome to romance.

Last year, I requested your opinions on the books that we publish. Thank you for the many thoughtful comments. For the next few months, I'd like to share quotes with you from those letters. This seems very appropriate while we are in the midst of the THAT SPECIAL WOMAN! promotion. Each one of our readers is a **special** woman, as heroic as the heroines in our books.

Our THAT SPECIAL WOMAN! title for October is *On Her Own* by Pat Warren. This is a heroine to cheer for as she returns to her hometown and the man she never forgot.

Also in store for you in October is *Marriage Wanted,* the third book in Debbie Macomber's heartwarming trilogy, FROM THIS DAY FORWARD. And don't miss *Here Comes the Groom* by Trisha Alexander, a spin-off from her *Mother of the Groom.*

Rounding out the month are books from Marie Ferrarella, Elizabeth Bevarly and Elyn Day, who makes her Silhouette Debut as Special Edition's PREMIERE author.

I hope you enjoy this book, and all of the stories to come!

Sincerely,

Tara Gavin
Senior Editor

QUOTE OF THE MONTH:

"I'm the mother of six, grandmother of ten and a registered nurse. I work in a hospice facility and deal with death and dying forty hours a week. Romance novels, light and airy, are my release from the stress."

L. O'Donnell
Maine

DEBBIE MACOMBER

MARRIAGE WANTED

SPECIAL V EDITION®

Published by Silhouette Books New York

America's Publisher of Contemporary Romance

If you purchased this book without a cover you should be aware that this book is stolen property. It was reported as "unsold and destroyed" to the publisher, and neither the author nor the publisher has received any payment for this "stripped book."

For
Theresa Scott
The best is yet to come!

SILHOUETTE BOOKS
300 East 42nd St., New York, N.Y. 10017

MARRIAGE WANTED

Copyright © 1993 by Debbie Macomber

All rights reserved. Except for use in any review, the reproduction or utilization of this work in whole or in part in any form by any electronic, mechanical or other means, now known or hereafter invented, including xerography, photocopying and recording, or in any information storage or retrieval system, is forbidden without the permission of the publisher, Silhouette Books, 300 E. 42nd St., New York, N.Y. 10017

ISBN: 0-373-09842-1

First Silhouette Books printing October 1993

All the characters in this book have no existence outside the imagination of the author and have no relation whatsoever to anyone bearing the same name or names. They are not even distantly inspired by any individual known or unknown to the author, and all incidents are pure invention.

®: Trademark used under license and registered in the United States Patent and Trademark Office and in other countries.

Printed in the U.S.A.

Books by Debbie Macomber

DEBBIE MACOMBER

hails from the state of Washington. As a busy wife and mother of four, she strives to keep her family healthy and happy. As the prolific author of dozens of best-selling romance novels, she strives to keep her readers happy with each new book she writes.

Dear Friends,

Marriage of convenience is a plot line that fascinates me. I've read hundreds of books that use this device and never get tired of them. Apparently, other romance readers feel the same way. For the last book of this trilogy, I wanted to create a special story with special characters. I believe *Marriage Wanted* is my personal favorite, although it's difficult to choose.

Savannah Charles is a sensitive, fanciful romantic. She owns and operates a wedding shop. Dash Davenport is a divorce attorney who gave up on love and marriage years earlier. But you know what they say about opposites attracting. Savannah and Dash are meant for each other, but neither of them is willing to admit it.

As it happens, marriage would be advantageous for them. Savannah knows Dash has the power to break her heart, and she can't give him that much control over her life. Dash doesn't need a woman clouding his head with talk of romance and love. And yet . . . yet there's something about Savannah he needs.

Dash learns a whole lot from this incredible woman before the story ends. Savannah is something special, but then so is Dash. A note of interest: the vows Dash and Savannah share are the ones I wrote for the wedding of my daughter Jenny and her husband, Kevin, last August.

Thank you for reading the last book in the FROM THIS DAY FORWARD trilogy. It's been fun, hasn't it? Remember to keep love alive in your own life; give it away each and every day and it will be returned to you a hundredfold, sometimes from the most unexpected sources.

I love to hear from my readers and I'd love to know how you liked this trilogy. You can write to me at P.O. Box 1458, Port Orchard, WA 98366.

Warmest regards,

Debbie Macomber

Chapter One

Savannah Charles had seen others like her. The young woman who'd come into her bridal shop moments earlier wandered about, checking prices, looking more discouraged by the moment. Her shoulders slumped and she bit into her lower lip when she read the tag on the wedding gown she'd selected. She had excellent taste, Savannah granted her that much. The ivory silk-taffeta dress was one of her personal favorites. A pattern of lace, pearls and sequins swirled up the puffed sleeves and bodice.

"Can I help you?" Savannah asked, ambling toward her. Startled, the woman turned around. "I . . . It doesn't look like it. This wedding dress alone is almost twice as much as my wedding budget for the whole wedding. Are you Savannah?"

"Yes."

She smiled shyly. "Missy Gilbert told me about you. She said you're wonderful to work with and that you might be able to help Kurt and me. I'm Susan Davenport." She held out her hand and Savannah shook it, liking the girl immediately.

"When's your wedding?"

"Six weeks. Kurt and I are paying for it ourselves. His two younger brothers are still in college and his parents can't afford to give us much help." Amusement turned up the soft corners of her mouth as she added, "Kurt's dad claims he's going poor in degrees."

"What about your family?"

"There's only my brother and me. He's fifteen years older and, well . . . it isn't that he doesn't like Kurt. Once you meet Kurt, it'd be impossible not to love him. He's really wonderful."

Young love, Savannah mused. Her heart was touched by Susan's eagerness to tell her about the man she wanted to marry.

"You see, Dash doesn't believe in marriage," the young woman went on to explain. "He's an attorney and has worked on so many divorce cases over the years that he simply doesn't believe in the institution of marriage anymore. It doesn't help any that he's divorced himself, although that was years and years ago now."

"What's your budget?" Savannah asked. She'd planned weddings that went into six figures, but she was equally adept at being cost-effective. She walked back to her desk, limping on her right foot. It ached more this afternoon than usual. It always did when the humidity was this high.

Susan told her the figure she and Kurt had managed to set aside and Savannah frowned. It wasn't much, but it was workable. She turned around and found Susan staring at her. Savannah was accustomed to people's reaction to her mangled leg. Until they knew her better, her handicap seemed to disconcert them. Generally she chose to ignore their hesitation and continue, hoping that her acceptance of her impediment would put them at ease within a few moments.

"Even the least expensive wedding dresses would eat up the majority of the money we've worked so hard to save."

"You could always rent the dress," Savannah suggested.

"I could?" Her pretty blue eyes lit up when Savannah mentioned the rental fee.

"How many are you planning to invite?"

"Sixty-seven," Susan told her, as if this number had been painfully difficult to pare down to. "Kurt and I can't afford more. Mostly it's his family.... I don't think Dash will even come to the wedding." Her voice dipped, as if voicing her suspicion pained her.

Savannah had never met Susan's older brother, but already she disliked him. From what little she'd heard, the man was an unreasonable bore. Savannah couldn't imagine a brother refusing to attend his own sister's wedding, no matter what his personal views on marriage happened to be.

"Kurt's from a large family. He has aunts and uncles and I swear a thousand or more cousins. We'd like to invite everyone, but we simply can't afford it. The invitations alone will cost plenty."

"Have you thought about making your own invitations?"

Susan shook her head. "I'm not very artsy."

"You don't need to be." Opening a drawer, Savannah brought out a book with several illustrations. "These are simple and elegant looking and add a personal touch because they're individualized."

"They're beautiful. You honestly think I could do this?" She looked expectantly at Savannah.

"Without a doubt," Savannah answered with a smile.

"I wish I could talk some sense into Dash," Susan muttered, then squared her shoulders as if she was ready to take him on right that minute. "He's the only family I have. We've got an aunt and uncle here and there, but no one we're close to, and Dash's being so unreasonable about this. I love Kurt and nothing's going to change the way I feel. I love his family, too. It can be lonely when you don't belong to someone. That's Dash's problem, more than anything else. He's forgotten what it's like to belong to someone."

Loneliness. Savannah was well acquainted with the feeling. It was a cry that came from the darkest recesses of her soul. The little girl who couldn't run and play with her friends. The teenage girl who never got asked to the prom. The woman who arranged the happiest days of other people's lives.

Loneliness. Savannah knew all she wanted to about long days and longer nights. She knew all she wanted about silent phones and empty mailboxes.

"I'm sure your brother will change his mind," Savannah said reassuringly.

Susan laughed. "That only goes to prove you don't know my brother. Once he's got his mind set on something, it takes an Act of Congress to persuade him otherwise."

Savannah spent the next hour with Susan, discussing the details of the wedding and reception. With such a limited budget it was a challenge, but they did it.

"I can't believe we can do so much," Susan said once they'd finished. Her face glowed with happiness. "A nice wedding doesn't mean nearly as much to Kurt as it does to me, but he's willing to do whatever he can to make our special day memorable."

Through the course of their conversation, Savannah learned that Kurt had recently graduated from the University of Washington with an engineering degree. Briefly Savannah wondered what it was about the young man that her brother found so objectionable. Kurt had recently been hired by a California firm and had moved to the San Francisco area.

After defying her brother, Susan had moved in with Kurt's family, working part-time and saving every penny she could to help with the wedding expenses.

"I can hardly wait to talk to Kurt," Susan said excitedly as she gathered her purse and the variety of notes she'd made. "I'll get back to you as soon as he's had a chance to go over the contract." Susan hesitated. "Missy was right, you're wonderful." Savannah found herself wrapped in Susan's arms for an impulsive hug. "I'll be back as soon as I can and you can take the measurements for the dress." She cast a dreamy look toward the silk-and-taffeta gown and sighed audibly. "Kurt's going to die when he sees me in that dress."

"You'll make a lovely bride."

"Thank you so much," Susan said, walking backward toward the door.

"You're most welcome." It was helping young women like Susan that Savannah enjoyed the most. The eager, happy ones who were so much in love they were willing to listen to their hearts no matter what the cost. Over the years, Savannah had worked with every kind of bride and she knew the signs. The Susans of this world were a delight.

It was highly unlikely that Savannah would ever be married herself. Men were an enigma to her. Try as she might, she never had been able to understand them. The opposite sex invariably treated her differently than they did other women. Savannah assumed their attitude had to do with her damaged leg. Men viewed her as a buddy, a confidante, a trusted friend. She supposed she should be flattered by the easy camaraderie they shared with her. They sought her advice, listened politely when she spoke, then did as they damn well pleased.

Over the years, only a few brave souls had viewed her as a woman with dreams and desires of her own, but when it came to loving her, really loving her, they'd grown hesitant and afraid. Each relationship had ended awkwardly long before it had gotten close to serious.

That wasn't a fair assessment, Savannah mused sadly. She'd been terrified of ever falling in love. No matter how strongly she felt toward a man, she was positive her imperfection would eventually stand between them. It was safer to hold on to her pride than risk rejection and pain later.

Savannah didn't see Susan again for a week. The twenty-one-year-old came breezing through the door to Savannah's shop like a tumbleweed skipping across the roadway.

"Hello," she greeted, smiling broadly. "I talked to Kurt and he's as excited as I am." She withdrew her checkbook from her purse. "I'd like to give you the down payment now, if that would be all right. You were so helpful, Savannah, I can't thank you enough."

Savannah brought out her paperwork and Susan wrote out the check and ripped it free. "My brother doesn't believe I'll be able to do it without his help, but he's wrong. I'm going to have a beautiful wedding, with or without Dash, thanks to you."

It was helping clients like Susan that made Savannah's job so fulfilling. "I'll order what we need right away," she assured Susan. Savannah only wished there were something she could do about the young woman's unreasonable older brother. She knew his type well: cynical, distrusting, pessimistic. A man who scoffed at love, a man who had no respect for the institution of marriage. How very sad. Despite her irritation with the faceless Dash, Savannah couldn't help feeling sorry for him. He was going to lose his sister. The poor man didn't stand a chance, not in the face of young love.

As there was only the two of them, it would help if Dash supported his sister in her decision, Savannah mused. Luckily Susan had Kurt's parents. Undoubtedly this was something her brother hadn't counted on, as well.

Susan left soon afterward. What remained of Savannah's day was busy. It used to be the summer months were her overburdened time of the year, but that hadn't held true of late. Her services were booked equally throughout the year.

Around five-thirty, just when Savannah was getting ready to close for the day, the bell chimed over her door, indicating someone had entered her shop. She looked up from her position at her desk and found a tall, well-dressed man standing just inside the doorway. He glanced around, and frowned as if being in such a place was repugnant to him. Even before he spoke she knew he was Susan's brother. The family resemblance was striking.

"Hello," she said.

"Hello." He stuffed his hands in his pockets. He glanced around with a contemptuous frown, as though he feared even being in this place where love and romance were honored would infect him with some serious disease. It must take a good deal of energy to maintain his cynicism, Savannah thought, and almost felt sorry for him. Almost. "Can I help you?"

"No, thanks. I was just looking." He slowly wandered about the shop. His expensive leather shoes made clicking sounds against the polished hardwood floor. She noticed that he took pains not to touch anything.

Savannah nearly laughed out loud when he passed a display of satin pillows, edged in French lace, that were meant to be carried by the ring bearer. He stepped out of its way, making a wide circle around the arrangement. He picked up one of her business cards from a brass holder on an small antique table where she worked with clients.

"Are you Savannah Charles?" he asked.

"Yes," she replied evenly.

"This is an interesting shop you have here," he commented dryly. On first look Savannah found him handsome in a rugged sort of way. His facial features were strong and well-defined. His mouth firm, his jaw square and stubbornly set. He walked in short, clipped steps, his impatience nearly palpable. It was as though he were standing in front of the jury box. Naturally, she might be off base altogether and this could be someone other than Susan's brother. Savannah decided it was time to test the waters.

"Are you about to be married?"

"No," he said disgustedly. "Hell, no!" he added with heavy emphasis on both words.

"This seems an unusual shop for you to browse through, then."

He smiled in her direction, reluctantly acknowledging her shrewdness. "I believe you've been talking to my sister, Susan Davenport."

So Savannah had been right. This was Susan's hard-nosed older brother. His attitude had been a dead giveaway. "Yes, Susan's been in."

"I take it she's decided to go through with this wedding business, then?" He eyed her suspiciously as if to suggest his sister might have changed her mind without Savannah's encouragement and support.

"It would be best if you discussed Susan's plans with her."

Dash clasped his hands behind his back. "I would if we were on speaking terms."

How he knew his sister was working with her, Savannah hadn't a clue. She didn't even want to know.

"So," he said conversationally, "exactly what kind of business do you have here?"

"I'm a wedding coordinator."

"Wedding coordinator," he repeated, sounding genuinely curious. He cocked his head to one side for her to continue.

"Basically I organize the wedding for the bride and her family so they're free to enjoy this all-important day."

"I see," he said as a matter of course. "You're the one who makes sure the flowers arrive at the church on time?"

"Something like that." His version grossly simplified her role, but she didn't think he'd appreciate a detailed job description. After all, he wasn't interested in her, but what he could learn about his sister and Kurt's plans.

He wandered about the shop some more, taking pains not to come in contact with any of the displays she'd so carefully arranged about the cramped space. He strolled past a lace-covered table with an elegant heart-shaped guest book and plumed pen as if he were walking past a mine field. Savannah couldn't help being amused by his attitude.

"Susan hasn't got the money for any kind of wedding," he announced sharply. "At least, not one fancy enough to hire a coordinator."

"Again, this is something you need to discuss with your sister."

He didn't like her answer, that much was obvious from the way his mouth thinned and the irritation that glowed from his strong facial features. His eyes were the same intense blue as his sister's, but that was where the comparison stopped. Susan's eyes revealed her love and her enthusiasm for life. Dash's revealed his disenchantment and skepticism. She continued finishing up the last of her paperwork, ignoring him as much as she could.

"You're a babe in the woods, aren't you?"

"I beg your pardon?" Savannah said, looking up.

"You actually believe all this bull."

"I certainly don't think of love and commitment as bull, if that's what you mean, Mr. Davenport."

"Call me Dash."

"All right," she agreed reluctantly. In a few minutes she was going to be showing him the door. He hadn't bothered to disguise the purpose of his visit. He was looking to pump her for information and had yet to realize that she refused to be placed in the middle between him and his sister.

"Did you ever stop to realize that over fifty percent of the couples who marry in this day and age end up divorcing?"

"I know the statistics, if that's what you're asking."

He walked purposely toward her as if approaching a judge's bench, intent on proving his point. "Love is a lame excuse for marriage."

Seeing that he was going to make it impossible for her to concentrate, she sat back on her stool and folded her arms. "What do you suggest couples do then, Mr. Davenport? Live together?"

"Dash," he reminded her irritably. "And, yes, living together makes a hell of a lot of sense. If a man and a woman are so hot for each other, I don't see any reason to muddy up the relationship with marriage when a weekend in bed would simplify everything."

Savannah resisted the urge to roll her eyes. That made as much sense to her as driving a car over a cliff because the fender was dented. Instead she asked, "Is

this what you want Susan and Kurt to do? Live together without commitment?''

That gave him pause. Apparently it was perfectly
fine for other couples to do as he suggested, but when
it came to his little sister, he hesitated. ''Yes,'' he said
finally. ''Until this infatuation passes.''

''What about children?'' she asked, openly curious
about his views on the subject.

''Susan's little more than a child herself,'' he argued, then seemed to realize that his twenty-one-year-
old sister could make her own decisions. Indeed she
had been doing exactly that. ''If she's smart, she'll
avoid adding to her mistakes,'' he answered stiffly.

''What about someone other than your sister?'' she
demanded, irritated with herself as much as him for
allowing him to draw her into this pointless discussion. ''Are you suggesting that our society does away
with family as we know it?''

''A wedding ring doesn't make a family,'' he returned just as heatedly.

Savannah sighed deeply. ''I think it's best for us to
agree to disagree,'' she said, feeling a bit sad. It was
unrealistic to think she'd say anything that would
change his mind about any of this. Susan was determined to marry Kurt, with or without his approval,
but she loved her brother, too. That was what made
this situation so difficult.

''Love is a lame excuse to mess up one's life,'' he
said, clenching his fists at his side with impotent anger. ''A lame excuse.''

At his third unexpected use of the word *lame*, Savannah inwardly flinched. Because she was sitting behind her desk, he didn't realize she was crippled
herself.

"Marriage is an expensive trap that destroys a man's soul," Dash went on to say, ignoring her. "I see the results of it each and every day. Just this afternoon, I was in court for a settlement hearing that was so nasty the judge had to pull both attorneys into chambers. Do you honestly believe I want my little sister involved in something like that?"

"Your sister is a grown woman, Mr. Davenport. She's old enough to make her own decisions."

"Mistakes, you mean."

Savannah sensed his frustration, but arguing with him would do little good. "Susan's in love. You should have realized by now she's determined to marry Kurt."

"Love. Excuses don't get much worse than that."

Savannah had had enough. She stood and realized for the first time how tall Dash actually was. He loomed head and shoulders over her petite five-foot-three-inch frame. Standing next to him she felt small and insignificant. For all their differences, Savannah could appreciate his concerns. Dash loved his sister, otherwise he wouldn't have gone to such pains to find out her plans. Their conversation had both amused and angered her. For several moments, they'd played tag with the fuzzy differences between right and wrong, love and pain, and sadly had gained nothing.

"It's been interesting," Dash said, waiting for her to walk around her desk and join him. Savannah did, limping as she went. She was halfway across the room before she realized he wasn't following her. Half turning around, she noticed he was staring at her leg, his features riddled with regret.

"I meant no offense," he said, and she couldn't doubt his sincerity. What surprised her was his sensitivity. She may have judged this man too harshly. His attitude had irritated her no end, but by some odd quirk of nature she'd been equally amused.

"None was taken—you didn't know." She finished her trek to the door, again surprised to realize he hadn't followed her. "It's well past my closing time," she said meaningfully.

"Of course." His steps were crisp and uniform as he marched across her shop, stopping abruptly when he reached her. A frown marred his brow as he stared at her.

"Is something wrong?"

He laughed shortly. "I'm trying to figure something out."

"If it has to do with Susan and Kurt—"

"It doesn't," he cut in. "It has to do with you." An odd off-kilter smile lifted the edges of his mouth. "I like you. You're impertinent, sassy and stubborn."

"Oh, really!" She might have been offended if she hadn't been struggling so hard not to laugh.

"Really."

"You're tactless, irritating and overpowering," she added.

His grin was transformed into a full-blown smile. "You're right. It's a damn shame, though."

Her leg—he was going to mention her leg, tell her what a beauty she would have been if she were a whole person. She held her breath in painful anticipation. "A shame?"

"You being a wedding coordinator. It's a waste, a pure waste of genius. With your organizational skills, you might have made something of your life. Instead, your head's stuck in the clouds and you've let love and romance fog up your brain. But you know something?" He hesitated and rubbed the side of his jaw as if analyzing his thoughts. "There just might be hope for you."

"Hope. Funny, I was thinking the same thing about you. There just might be a slim chance of reasoning with you. It's apparent you're intelligent and more than a little witty. But unfortunately you're terribly misguided. Now that you're dealing with your sister, there's a remote possibility someone might be able to reason with you."

"What do you mean?" he asked, folding his arms over his muscular chest and resting his weight on one foot.

"Your judgment's been clouded with your clients' estrangements, bitterness and separations. We're working from opposite ends of the same subject. I work with couples when they're deeply in love and convinced their relationship will last forever. You see them from the reverse perspective when they're embittered and disillusioned, but what you don't seem to realize is that the cup is half-full and not half-empty."

He frowned. "I thought we were talking about marriage. What do cups have to do with this?"

"What you said earlier is true, fifty percent of all married couples end up divorcing, which means fifty percent of them go on to lead fulfilling, happy lives."

Dash's snort was derisive. He dropped his arms and straightened, on the defensive. "I was wrong. There's no hope for you. The fifty percent that stay together are just as miserable. Given the opportunity, they'd gladly get out of the relationship."

Dash was beginning to irritate her again. "Why is it so difficult for you to accept that there's such a thing as a happy marriage?"

"Because I've yet to see one."

"You haven't looked hard enough."

"Have you ever stopped to think it might be that your head's so muddled with thoughts of hearts and flowers and happily-ever-afters that you can't and won't accept what's right before your eyes?"

"It's well past my closing time," Savannah said as she jerked open the shop door. Like a boxing match, the clanging bell marked the end of their frustrating conversation. Rarely had Savannah allowed anyone to get under her skin the way she had Dash Davenport. The man was impossible. Totally unreasonable...

The woman was impossible. Totally unreasonable.

What Dash couldn't understand was why he continued to mull over their conversation. Twenty-four hours had passed and he'd rehashed their verbal sparring match a dozen times or more.

Relaxing against the high back of his leather chair, he rolled a pen between his palms. Obviously Savannah didn't know him well; otherwise, she wouldn't have attempted to convince him of the error of his ways.

Like most women, Savannah Charles was deceptive, and that was where he'd made his mistake. She was no bigger than a minute, but she had the heart of a lion tamer.

His eyes fell on the phone and he sighed inwardly. Susan was being both stubborn and irrational. It was plain that he was going to have to be the one to mend fences between them. He'd hoped she'd come to her senses, but it was apparent that wasn't going to happen. He was her older brother, her closest relative and damn it all, he wished she had the common sense she was born with to listen to what he had to say. Damn fool woman!

He flipped through his phone book until he found Kurt Caldwell's parents' phone number. It tightened his jaws to contact her there. Luck was with him, however, when Susan answered herself.

"It's Dash," he said. When she was little, he remembered how her voice rose with excitement whenever he called. When he arrived home, she flew into his arms, so glad to see him she couldn't hold still. His sigh was weighted with sadness, missing the child she once was.

"Hello, Dash," Susan said stiffly. None of that pleasure to be hearing from him was there now.

"How are you doing?" That was the purpose of this call, after all.

"Fine. How about you?" How stilted she sounded, too stubborn for her own damn good, he decided. He would have said as much, then thought better of it. Years ago his mother had taught him it was easier to catch flies with honey than vinegar.

"I'm good, too," he answered.

The silence stretched between them.

"I understand you have a wedding coordinator now," he said, hoping to come across as vaguely interested. She might have defied him, but he would always be her big brother.

"How'd you know that?"

"Word gets around." He shouldn't have said anything about what he'd learned. He wouldn't have if Savannah hadn't dominated his thoughts from the moment he'd clashed with her.

"You've had someone checking into my affairs, haven't you?" Susan's voice dipped to subzero temperatures. "You can't rule my life, Dash. I'm going to marry Kurt and nothing you say will change my mind."

"I got that much from Savannah Charles...."

"You've talked to Savannah?"

Dash realized his second mistake immediately. He'd blown it royally now, and Susan wasn't going to forgive him without first drawing blood.

"Stop meddling in my life, Dash." His sister's voice wobbled suspiciously and a moment later the line was disconnected. The phone droned in his ear for a couple of moments before he dejectedly replaced the receiver.

Needless to say, that conversation hadn't gone well. He'd like to blame Savannah for that, as well, but he'd been the one to let her name slip. It was a stupid error on his part.

The wedding coordinator and his sister were both too damn stubborn and naive for their own good. If this was the way Susan wanted it, then he had no choice but to abide by her wishes. Contacting her had been a mistake in a long list he seemed bent on making of late.

His intercom buzzer beeped and his secretary's voice cut into his thoughts. He had more important matters to handle than his sister and a feisty wedding coordinator who lived in a dreamworld.

"What did my brother say?" Susan demanded of Savannah.

"He wanted to know about you," Savannah answered absently as she arranged the tulip-shaped champagne flutes on the display table next to the five-tier wedding cake. She'd been working on the display in between customers for the past hour.

"In other words, Dash was pumping you for information?"

"Yes, but you don't need to worry, I didn't tell him anything. What I did do was suggest he talk to you." She straightened, surprised that he'd followed her advice. "He deeply cares for you, Susan."

"I know." Susan gnawed on her lower lip. "I wish I hadn't hung up the phone on him."

"Susan!"

"I... He told me he'd talked to you and it made me so mad that I couldn't bear to speak to him another second."

Savannah was surprised by Dash's slip. She would have thought the last thing he'd let drop was the gist of their conversation. From the sounds of it, he didn't get the opportunity to rehash it with Susan.

"If he makes a pest of himself," Susan said righteously, "let me know and I'll... I'll do something."

"Don't worry about it. I rather enjoyed talking to him." It was true, although Savannah hated to admit it. She'd worked hard to push thoughts of Dash from her mind over the past couple of days. His attitude had annoyed her, true, but she'd found him intriguing and, it bothered her to confess to this, a challenge. A smile came when she realized he probably viewed her the same way.

"I have to get back to work," Susan said reluctantly. "I just wanted to apologize for my brother's behavior."

"He wasn't any problem."

On her way out the door, Susan muttered something under her breath that Savannah couldn't hear.

The situation was sad. It was apparent brother and sister deeply cared for one another but were at an impasse.

Savannah continued to mull over the situation until the bell over the door chimed no more than five minutes later. Smiling, she looked up, realizing she wasn't going to get this display finished until after closing time. She should have known better than to try.

"Dash." His name was a whisper on her lips, he surprised her so.

"Hello again," he said dryly. "I've come to prove my point beyond a shadow of a doubt."

Chapter Two

"You want to prove your point," Savannah repeated thoughtfully. Dash Davenport was the most headstrong man she'd ever encountered. He was also one of the handsomest. That thought did more to confuse her than help her thought processes. Generally she'd didn't view the opposite sex the way she did Dash. For reasons as yet unclear, she'd lost her objectivity. No doubt it had something to do with that stubborn pride of his and the way they continually butted heads. No doubt it was because they remained diametrically opposed on the most fundamental issues of life: love and marriage. No doubt it didn't make a damn bit of sense.

"I've been doing some heavy thinking about the course our conversation took the other day," Dash continued, pacing back and forth, unable to stand in one place for long, "and it seems to me that I'm just the person to clear up your thinking. Besides," Dash said, "if I can clear up your thinking, maybe you'll have some influence on Susan."

Although it was difficult, Savannah resisted the urge to laugh out loud.

"To prove my good faith, I brought along a peace offering." He held up a white sack for her inspection. "Two lattes," he explained. He set the bag on the corner of her desk and opened it, handing her one of the thick paper cups. The smell of hot coffee blended with steamed milk was as welcome as popcorn in a theater. "Make yourself comfortable," he said next, gesturing toward the stool, "because this might take some doing."

"I don't know that this is a good idea," Savannah felt obliged to say as she carefully edged herself onto a comfortable stool.

"It's a great idea. Just wait and hear me out," he countered smoothly.

"Oh, all right," she returned with an ungracious nod. Savannah might have had the energy to resist him if it hadn't been so late in the day. She was tired and the afternoon had frustrated her. Susan had come to her upset and unhappy and Savannah had felt helpless, not knowing what to say to ease the younger woman's mind.

Dash pried open the lid of his latte and paced in front of her stool as he continued to gather his thoughts, as if he had yet to put order to them. After a moment, he glanced at his watch, walked over to her door and turned over the sign so it read "Closed."

"I think it's only fair for you to know that whatever you have to say isn't going to change my mind,"

Savannah said, tapping her fingers against her forearm.

"I figured as much."

The man continued to surprise her. "What do you intend to do to prove your point? Parade divorced couples through my wedding shop?"

"Nothing that drastic."

"Did you stop to realize I could do the same thing and have you meet with several newlyweds?" she asked.

He grinned, looking relaxed and confident. "I'm way ahead of you. I figured you'd take delight in introducing me to any number of lovebirds who swoon at the mere sight of one another."

Savannah shrugged, not wanting him to realize that had been exactly what she was thinking.

"The way I figure it, we both have a strong argument to make."

"Exactly." She was in full agreement. "But you aren't going to change my mind and I doubt that I'll change yours." She couldn't answer her own questions about love and hate. She didn't know what it was that kept some couples together against all odds or why others decided to divorce and had to look for an excuse. If Dash was looking for her to supply the answers, she had none to offer.

"Don't be so sure we won't change the other's mind." Which only went to prove he thought there was a chance he would influence her. "We could accomplish a good deal if we each agree to be open-minded."

Savannah cocked her eyebrow and regarded him skeptically. "Can you guarantee you'll be open-minded?"

"I'm not sure," he answered, and she was impressed with his honesty. "But I'm willing to try. That's all I ask of you."

"That sounds fair."

He brightened and rubbed his palms together as though eager to get started. "If you don't object, I'd like to go first."

"Just a minute," she said, holding up her hand. "Before we get started, shouldn't we set some kind of rules?"

"Like what?"

Although it was her suggestion, Savannah wasn't sure what she meant. "I don't really know. Just boundaries of some kind."

"I trust you not to do anything weird, and you can expect the same thing from me," he said, clearly impatient to get started. "After all—"

"Don't be so hasty," she interrupted. "If we're going to put time and effort into this project, it makes sense we should have something riding on the outcome."

His blue eyes brightened at the prospect. "Now there's an interesting thought." He paused and a smile slowly leaked into his features, bracketing his mouth and his eyes with well-creased lines. "So you care to set a wager to this?"

Having second thoughts, Savannah shrugged her shoulders. Dash seemed to be on a one-man campaign to convince her the world would be a better place without the institution of marriage. "We might as well make this interesting, don't you think?"

"I couldn't agree more. If you can prove your point and get me to agree that you have, what would you want in exchange?"

This part was easy. "For you to attend Susan and Kurt's wedding. It would mean the world to Susan."

The easy smile disappeared behind a dark frown.

"She was in this afternoon," Savannah continued, rushing the words together in her eagerness to explain. "She's anxious and confused, loving you and loving Kurt and needing your approval so badly."

Dash's mouth narrowed into a thin line of irritation.

"Would it really be so much to ask?" she ventured. "I realize I'd need to rely on your complete and total honesty, but I have faith in you." She took a sip of her latte and glanced up at him expectantly.

"If you convince me my thinking is wrong on this marriage issue, you want me to attend Susan's wedding." He stated this without emotion, as if he had to say the words aloud to garner their meaning. He hesitated, then nodded sharply. "Deal," he said, and a slow grin meandered back into place.

Until that moment, Savannah was convinced Dash hadn't a clue about what he intended to use for his argument. Apparently he did. "What would you want from me?" she asked. Her question broke into his musings because he jerked his head toward her as if he'd forgotten there might be something in this for him, as well. He stared at her a couple of moments, blew up his cheeks with hot air and slowly released it. "I don't know. Do I have to decide that this moment?"

"No."

"It'll be something substantial—you realize that, don't you?"

Savannah managed to hold back a smile. "I wouldn't expect anything less."

"Home-cooked dinners for a week served on your fancy china wouldn't be out of line," he suggested, then nodded as if he'd labored hard over the decision.

So it was to be like that. Her request had been generous and completely selfless. She had offered him an excuse to attend Susan's wedding and salvage his pride, and in return he wanted her to slave in a kitchen for days on end.

"Dinner for a week served on expensive china is out of the question," she told him, unwilling to agree to anything so ridiculous. If he wanted homemade meals, he could do what the rest of the world did and cook them himself, visit relatives or get married.

Dash's returning grin was boyish with delight. "So you're afraid you're going to lose."

Holding back a snicker would have required a miracle. "You haven't got a prayer, Davenport."

"Then what's the problem?" he asked with an exaggerated gesture of both hands. "Do you agree to my terms or not?"

This discussion had wandered far from what she'd originally intended. Savannah had been looking for a way to smooth matters between brother and sister and at the same time prove her own point. She wasn't looking to put her own neck on the chopping block. The idea of convincing Dash of the error of his ways was pointless.

Dash finished off the last of his latte, and with a sporty toss flung the empty container into her garbage receptacle. "Be ready tomorrow afternoon," he said on his way toward the door.

Savannah awkwardly scooted from her perch on the stool. "What for?" she called after him. She limped two steps toward him and stopped abruptly at the flash of pain that shot up her leg. She'd sat too long in the same position, something she was generally able to avoid. She longed to rub her thigh, work the throbbing muscle, but to do so would reveal her pain and she wanted to hide that from Dash.

"You'll know more tomorrow afternoon," he promised, looking pleased with himself.

"How long will this take?"

"There are time restrictions?" His voice dipped as though he was disappointed in her for asking. "Are there any other rules we need to discuss?"

"I... We should both be reasonable about this, don't you think?" He had a way of making her feel foolish with a simple angle of his eyebrow.

"I was planning on being sensible about all this, but I can't speak for you."

This conversation was deteriorating rapidly. "I'll be ready at closing time tomorrow afternoon, then," she said, holding her hand against her thigh. If he didn't leave soon, she was going to have to sit down. Disguising her pain had become a way of life, but the longer she stood, the more difficult it became.

"Something's wrong," he announced, his gaze hard and steady. "You'd argue with me if there weren't."

Again she was impressed by his sensitivity. "Nonsense. I said I'd be ready. What more do you want?"

He left her then, in the nick of time. A low moan escaped as she eased her weight onto her chair. Perspiration moistened her brow and her hands trembled as she drew in several deep breaths. Rubbing her hand over the tense muscles slowly eased out the pain.

The phone was situated to the left of her desk and after giving the last of the discomfort a couple of moments to ebb away, she reached for the receiver and dialed her parents' number. Apparently Dash had decided how to present his case. She had, too. No greater argument could be made than her parents' loving relationship. Their marriage was as solid as Fort Knox and they had been devoted to one another for over thirty years. Dash couldn't meet her family and continue to discredit love and marriage.

Her father answered on the second ring, sounding delighted to hear from her. A warm rush of good feelings washed over Savannah. Her family had been a constant source of love and encouragement to her through the years.

"Hi, Dad."

"It's always good to hear from you, sweetheart."

Savannah relaxed against the back of her chair. "Is Mom around?"

"No, she's got a doctor's appointment to have her blood pressure checked again. Is there anything I can do for you?"

Savannah's hand tightened around the receiver. She didn't want to mislead her parents into thinking she was involved with Dash. But at the same time she needed to prove her point. "Is there any chance I could bring someone over for dinner tomorrow night?"

"Of course."

Savannah laughed lightly and the gay sound echoed into the receiver. "You might want to check Mom's calendar. It'd be just like you to agree to something when she's already made plans."

"I looked. The calendar's right here in the kitchen and tomorrow night's free, as far as I can see. Now if you were to ask about Friday, that's a different story."

Once more Savannah found herself smiling.

"Who is it you want us to meet?"

"His name's Dash Davenport."

Her announcement was met with a short, but noticeable, silence. "You're bringing a young man home to meet your family? This is something of an occasion, then."

"Dad, it isn't like that." This was exactly what she'd feared would happen, that her family would misinterpret her bringing Dash home. "We've only just met...."

"It happened like that with your mother and me," her father said excitedly. "We met on a Friday night and a week later I knew this was the woman I was going to love all my life, and I have."

"Dad, Dash is just a friend—not even a friend, really, just an acquaintance," Savannah said, trying to correct his mistaken impression. "I'm coordinating his sister's wedding."

"It's not necessary to explain, sweetheart. If you want to bring a young man for your mother and me to meet, we'd be delighted, no matter what the reason."

Savannah's mouth was poised open, her mind riddled with indecision. A lengthy explanation might hurt her cause rather than help her. "I'm not sure of the exact time we'll arrive."

"No problem. I'll light up the barbecue and that way you won't need to worry about dinner drying out in the oven. Come whenever you can and we'll make an evening of it."

It was going to prove to be an incredible night all right, Savannah mused darkly. Two stubborn people, each convinced they were right, were about to attempt to convince the other of the error of their thinking.

This was going to be so easy that Dash almost felt guilty. Almost, but not quite. Poor Savannah. Once he finished with what he had to show her, she had no option but to accept the reality of his argument. Given another set of circumstances, he might feel sorry for her.

Not this time, however. Dash loved this kind of debate, when he was convinced beyond a shadow of a doubt that he was right. By the time he'd finished, Savannah would be eating her words.

Grabbing his briefcase, he hurried out of his office, anxious to forge ahead and prove his point.

"Dash, what's the big hurry?"

Groaning inwardly, Dash turned around to face a fellow attorney, Paul Justice. "I've got an appointment this evening," Dash explained. He didn't like Paul, had never liked Paul. What plagued him most was that this brownnoser was going to be chosen over him for the partnership position that was opening up in the firm within the year. Both Paul and Dash had come into the firm at the same time, and they were both damn good attorneys. But Paul had a way of ingratiating himself with the powers that be and parting the waters of opportunity.

"An appointment or a date?" Paul asked with that smug look of his. One of these days Dash was going to find an excuse to wipe that grin off his peer's face. Unfortunately that time wasn't now.

Dash looked pointedly at his watch. "If you'll excuse me, I have to rush, otherwise I'll be late."

"We can't keep the little woman waiting, now can we?" Paul said, and finding himself amusing, he laughed at his own sorry joke.

Knotting his fist at his side, Dash was happy for the excuse to get away. Anger clawed at him until he was forced to stop and to analyze his outrage. He'd been working with Paul for nearly ten years now. He'd tolerated his humorless jokes, his conceited, self-righteous attitude and his air of superiority without displaying his annoyance. What was different now?

He rolled the idea of Paul being chosen above him for the partnership in his mind, letting it gain weight with each pass.

This wasn't something new. The minute he'd learned about the opening, he suspected Stackhouse and Sterle would choose Paul. He'd accepted it as fact weeks earlier.

Little woman. The phrase caught on the edges of his awareness like a thread against a hangnail. Paul had suggested Dash was hurrying to meet a woman, which he was. Dash didn't bother to deny the fact. It was the way Paul had said it, as though Savannah—

His mind went to a grinding halt. Savannah.

So she was at the bottom of all this. Dash had taken offense at the edge in Paul's voice, as if his fellow attorney had suggested Savannah was something less than what she should be. He knew he was being overly sensitive. After all, Paul had never even met Savannah. But still, Paul would be just the type to discredit her because of her handicap, and that irritated Dash.

She was small, Dash admitted. Her dark, pixie-style hair and deep brown eyes gave her a fragile, Tinker-bell appearance, but that was deceptive. The woman had a constitution of iron.

Her eyes ... Once more his thoughts skidded to a stop. He'd never known a woman with eyes that were more revealing. In them he read a multitude of emotions. Pain beyond description, both physical and emotional. In them he saw a woman with pluck and courage. Dash barely knew Savannah and yet he sensed she was one of the most astonishing persons he was ever likely to meet. He'd wanted to defend her, wanted to slam his colleague up against a wall and demand an apology for the slight, whether intentional or not.

When he reached his car, Dash sat in the driver's seat with his key poised in front of the ignition. His reaction wasn't justified, he realized. Paul didn't even know Savannah, and any insult was aimed directly in his direction and not hers.

His mood lightened considerably as he made his way through the heavy traffic to the wedding shop. He'd been looking forward to this meeting all day.

He found a parking spot and climbed out of his car and fed the meter three quarters. As he turned away he caught sight of Savannah in the shop window, talking to a customer. Her face was aglow with enthusiasm and even from this distance her eyes sparkled like the sun cutting across a row of diamond chips. For a reason unknown to him, his pulse accelerated as a surge of joy rushed through him.

He was happy to be seeing Savannah. Anyone would be, knowing they were about to be proven right, he told himself. But this was more than the obvious. This gladness that overcame him was rooted in the knowledge that he'd be spending time with her.

Savannah must have felt his scrutiny, because she glanced upward and their eyes met briefly before she reluctantly pulled hers away. Although she continued speaking to her customer, Dash realized she'd experienced the same intensity of feeling as he had. It was moments such as this that he wished he were privy to a woman's thoughts. He would have gladly forfeited their bet to know if she was as surprised and puzzled as he felt. Dash couldn't pinpoint the feeling; all he knew was that it made him uncomfortable. Damned uncomfortable.

The customer was leaving just as Dash entered the shop. Savannah was sitting down at her desk and intuitively he realized she needed to sit periodically because of her leg. She looked fragile at that moment, and confused. When she raised her eyes to meet his, he was surprised by the strength of her smile.

"You're right on time," she said.

"You would be, too, if you were about to have home-cooked meals personally served to you for the next week."

"Don't count on it, Counselor."

"Count on it," he repeated and laughed. "I've already got the menu chosen. We'll start out the first night with broiled New York-cut sirloin steak with French potatoes and a three-layer chocolate cake."

"How you love to dream," she said with an effortless laugh. "I find it amusing that you never stopped to ask if I could cook. I don't suppose anyone's mentioned your chauvinistic attitude, have they? It'll probably come as a surprise to learn that not all women are proficient in a kitchen. If by some odd quirk of fate you do happen to win this wager, you'll dine on boxed macaroni and cheese for seven days and like it."

Dash was stunned. She was right; he'd assumed she could cook as well as she managed everything else. Her shop was a testament to her talent, appealing to the eye in every aspect. True, it reeked of love and romance, of lace and pearls, of wedding gowns and satin pillows, but it had a homey, comfortable feel, as well. This wasn't an easy thing to admit. A wedding shop was the last place on this earth Dash ever thought would relax him.

"Are you ready to admit defeat?" he asked, making himself at home.

"Never, but before we get started I need to make a couple of phone calls. Do you mind?"

"Not in the least." He was a patient man, and never more so than now. The longer they delayed, the better. It wasn't likely Paul would stay late; he seldom if ever did. Dash wanted to avoid introducing Savannah to the other man. More important, he wanted her to himself. The thought came unbidden and unwelcome. This wasn't a date and he had no romantic interest in Savannah Charles, he reminded himself.

Savannah reached for the phone and he wandered around the shop noticing small displays he'd missed on his prior sojourns. On his first visit he'd felt as nervous as a naked man in a sorority house. He didn't know what he was expecting from a wedding coordinator, but certainly not the practical, gutsy woman he'd found.

He purposely trained his ears not to listen in on her conversation, but the crisp, businesslike tone of her voice was surprisingly captivating.

It was happening again—that disturbing feeling was back, deep in the pit of his stomach. He'd felt it before, several years earlier, and it had damn near ruined his life. He was in trouble here. Deep trouble. Panic shot through his blood and he felt the nearly overwhelming urge to turn and run in the opposite direction. The last time he'd experienced this feeling, he'd gotten married.

"I'm ready," Savannah said, and stood.

Dash stared at her for a long moment as his brain processed what was happening to him.

"Dash?"

He gave himself a hard mental shake. He didn't know what was happening, but he didn't like whatever it was. "Do you mind riding with me?" he asked, once he'd composed himself.

"That'll be fine."

The drive back to his office building in downtown Seattle was spent in relative silence. Savannah seemed to sense his reflective mood. Another woman would have attempted to fill the space with idle chatter. Dash was grateful she didn't.

After he'd parked, he led Savannah into his building and up the elevator to the law firm. She seemed impressed with the plush furnishings and the lavish view of Mount Rainier and Puget Sound from his twentieth-story window.

When she entered his office she walked directly to the window and set her purse on his polished oak credenza. "How do you manage to work with a view like this?" she asked, her voice soft with awe. Her gaze seemed mesmerized by the beauty that appeared before her.

After several years Dash had become immune to its splendor, but lately he found himself soaking up the solace he found there. He soon discovered that the color of the sky reflected like a mirror upon the water's surface. On a gray and hazy morning, the water was a dull shade of steel. When the sun shone, Puget Sound was a deep, iridescent greenish blue. He enjoyed studying the ferries and other commercial and pleasure craft as they intersected the waterways. More times than he could count, he had stood in the same spot as Savannah and sorted through his thoughts.

"It's all so beautiful," she said, turning back to him. Watching her standing in the same spot he had so often stood himself and hearing her give voice to his own feelings felt oddly comforting. The sooner he presented his argument, the better. The sooner he said what had to be said and put this woman out of his mind, the better.

"You ready?" he asked, flinging opening a file cabinet and withdrawing a handful of thick folders from the top drawer.

"As ready as I'll ever be," she said, helping herself to a chair on the other side of his desk.

Dash slapped the files down on the credenza, the sound echoing around the office like a gunshot. "Let's start with Adams versus Adams," he suggested, flipping through the pages of the top folder. "Now this was an interesting case. Married ten years, two boys. Then Martha learned that Bill was having an affair with a co-worker and so she decided to have one herself, only she chose a nineteen-year-old. The child-custody battle lasted two months, destroyed them financially and ended so bitterly that Bill moved out and hasn't been heard from since. The last I heard, Martha was clinically depressed and in and out of hospitals."

Savannah gasped. "What about the boys?" she asked once she'd recovered. "What happened to them?"

"Eventually they went to live with a relative. From what I understand, they're both in counseling and have been for the last couple of years."

"How very sad," Savannah whispered.

"Don't kid yourself, this is only the beginning. I'm starting with the *A*s and working my way through the file drawer. Let me know when you've had enough." He reached for a second folder. "Anderson versus Anderson... Ah, yes, I remember this one. She attempted suicide three times, blackmailed him emotionally, used the children as weapons, wiped him out financially and then sued for divorce, claiming he was an unfit father." His back was as stiff as his voice, which grew colder and darker as he continued outlining the case. He tossed aside that file and reached for another.

"Allison versus Allison," he continued crisply. "By the way, you should know I'm changing the names to protect the guilty."

"The guilty?"

"To my way of thinking, each participant in these cases made a mistake."

"You're about to suggest that their first error was falling in love."

"No," he returned coldly, "it all started with the wedding vows. No two people should be expected to live up to that ideal. It isn't humanly possible."

"You're wrong, Dash. People live up to those vows each and every day in small and large ways."

Dash jabbed his finger against the thick stack of folders. "This says otherwise. Love isn't meant to last.

Couples are kidding themselves if they think commitment lasts past the next morning. Life's like that and it's time the rest of the world woke up and smelled the coffee.''

"Oh, please!" Savannah cried, standing. She walked over to the window, her back to him, and clenched and unclenched her fists. Dash wondered if she was aware of the action, and doubted that she was.

"Own up, Savannah. Marriages don't work anymore. They haven't in years. The institution is outdated. If you want to stick your head in the sand, then fine. But when others stand to get hurt, that's when someone needs to clear the air." His voice rose once more with the heat of his argument.

Slowly Savannah turned around and stared at him. He must have been more spirited than he realized, because an odd, almost pitying look came over her.

"She must have hurt you very badly." Savannah's voice was so low, he had to strain to hear.

"Hurt me? What the hell are you talking about?"

She shook her head as though she was unaware she'd spoken out loud. "Your ex-wife."

The anger that burned through Dash was like an acid searing his soul. "Who told you about Denise?" he demanded.

"No one," she returned quickly.

He slammed closed the top file and stuffed the stack of folders back inside the drawer with little care and less concern. "How'd you know I was once married?"

"I'm sorry, Dash, I shouldn't have mentioned it."

"Who told you?" The answer was obvious but he wanted her to say it.

"Susan mentioned it...."

"How much did she tell you?"

"Just that it happened years ago." Each word revealed her reluctance to drag his sister into the conversation. "She wasn't breaking confidences, if that's what you think. I'm sure the only reason she mentioned it was to explain your—"

"I know why she mentioned it."

"I apologize, Dash. I shouldn't have said anything."

"Why not? My file's in another attorney's cabinet along with those of a thousand other fools just like me who were stupid enough to think love lasts."

Savannah continued to stare at him with those big round eyes of hers. "You loved her, didn't you?"

"As much as any foolish twenty-one-year-old loves anyone. Do you mind if we change the subject?"

"Susan's twenty-one."

"Exactly," he said, slapping his hand against the top of his desk. "And she's about to make the same foolish choice I did."

"But, Dash..."

"Have you heard enough, or do you need to listen to a few more cases?"

"I've heard enough."

"Good. Let's get out of here." The atmosphere in the office was stifling. It was as though each and every client he'd represented over the years had returned to remind him of the pain he'd lived through himself, only he'd come away smarter than most.

"Do you want me to drive you back to the office or would you prefer I take you home?" he asked, eager to be on his way.

"No," Savannah said as they walked out of the office. He purposely adjusted his steps to match her much slower gait. "If you don't mind, I'd prefer to have this whole issue settled this evening."

"That's fine with me." The sooner the better.

"If you don't mind, I'd like to head for my parents' home. I want you to meet them."

"Sure, why not?" he asked flippantly. His anger simmered just below the surface. This wasn't such a brilliant idea after all, he admitted.

Savannah gave him the address and offered directions. The drive on the freeway was slowed by the heavy traffic, which frustrated him even more. By the time they reached the exit, his nerves were frayed. He was about to suggest they do this another evening when she instructed him to take a left at the next light. They turned the corner, and a block and half down and were there.

They were walking toward the house when a tall, burly man with a thinning hairline came out the front door. "Savannah, sweetheart," he greeted. "So this is the young man you're going to marry."

Chapter Three

"Dad!" Savannah was mortified to the marrow of her bones. The heat leaked up from her neck to her cheeks, circling her ears.

Marcus Charles raised his hands, looking mystified. "Did I say something I shouldn't have?"

"I'm Dash Davenport," Dash said, offering Marcus his hand. In light of how her father had chosen to welcome Dash, his gesture was a generous one. She chanced a look in the attorney's direction and was relieved to find he was smiling.

"You'll have to forgive me for speaking out of turn," her father said, "but Savannah's never brought home a young man she wants us to meet."

"Daddy, that's not true."

"Name one," he challenged. "And while you're inventing a beau, I'll take Dash in and introduce him to your mother."

"Dad!"

"Hush now or you'll give Dash the wrong impression."

The wrong impression! If only he knew. This meeting couldn't have gotten off to a worse start, especially in Dash's present mood. She'd made a drastic mistake mentioning his marriage. It was more than obvious that he'd been badly hurt and was looking to put the memory behind him.

Dash had built a strong case against marriage. The more clients he mentioned, the harder edged his voice became. The grief of his own experience echoed in his voice as he listed the nightmares of the cases he'd represented.

Dash and her father were already in the house by the time Savannah walked up the stairs and into the living room. Her mother had redecorated the living room in a Southwestern motif, with painted clay pots and Navajo-style rugs. A recent addition was a pink plaster coyote with his neck raised, howling at the moon. In some ways that was what Savannah was doing—wailing at the impossible. The analogy wasn't lost on her.

Every time she viewed this room, Savannah experienced a twinge of sadness. Her mother loved the Southwest and her parents visited there often when her brother had lived in the area. Savannah knew her mother and father had once looked forward to moving south. She also knew she was the reason they hadn't. With her brother living in Texas and with no other immediate family living in the vicinity, they were uncomfortable leaving their daughter alone in the big city. Their crippled daughter.

A hundred times in the past few years, Savannah had attempted to convince them to go after their dreams, but they'd continually made excuses. They never came right out and said they remained in the Seattle area because of her. They didn't need to; in her heart she knew.

"Hi, Mom," Savannah said as she entered the kitchen. Her mother was standing at the sink, slicing tomatoes fresh from her garden. "Can I do anything to help?"

Joyce Charles set aside the knife and turned to give her a firm hug. "Savannah, let me look at you," she said, studying her. "You're working too hard again, aren't you?"

"Mom, I'm fine."

"Good. Now sit down here and have something cold to drink and tell me about Dash."

This was worse than Savannah first believed. She should have explained her purpose in bringing the attorney to meet her family in the very beginning, before introducing him. Giving them this wrong impression was bad enough, but she could only imagine what Dash was thinking.

When Savannah didn't immediately answer her question, Joyce supplied what information she already knew. "You're coordinating his sister's wedding and that's how you two met."

"Yes, but—"

"He really is handsome, sweetheart. What does he do?"

"He's an attorney," Savannah explained. "But Mom—"

"Just look at your dad." Laughing, Joyce motioned toward the kitchen window that looked out over the freshly mowed backyard. The barbecue was heating on the brick patio and her father was showing Dash his prize fishing flies. He'd been tying his own for years and took a good deal of pride in the craft.

After glancing out over the pair, Savannah sank into the kitchen chair. Her mother had already poured her a glass of lemonade. Her father displayed his fishing flies only when the guest was someone of importance, someone he was looking to impress. Savannah should have realized when she first mentioned Dash that her father had put the wrong connotation on this meeting.

"Mom," Savannah said, her hand circling the cold glass, "I think you should know Dash and I are friends. Nothing more."

"We know that, dear. Do you think he'll like my pasta salad? I added jumbo shrimp this time. I do so hope he's not a fussy eater."

Jumbo shrimp! So they were rolling out the red carpet. With her dad it was the fishing flies, with her mother it was her pasta salad. Sweet heaven, what had she let herself in for now?

"I'm sure Dash will enjoy your salad." As he would the home-cooked meals she'd be forced to serve him in the upcoming week. He'd gloat so much it wouldn't matter if he was eating boxed macaroni and cheese.

"Your father insisted on barbecuing steaks."

"T-bone," Savannah guessed.

"I think you might be right. I forget what he told me when he took them out of the freezer."

Savannah was growing more depressed by the minute.

"I thought we'd eat outside. You don't mind, do you, dear?"

"No, Mom, that'll be great." Nothing like a little sunshine to lift her spirits.

"Let's go on outside, then, shall we?" her mother suggested, carrying the large wooden bowl with the shrimp pasta salad with her.

The early-evening weather was perfect. The sun's rays warmed the earth and nature seemed to sigh in appreciation. Her mother's prize roses bloomed against the fence line. The bright red ones were Savannah's favorite. The flowering rhododendron tree cast its pink limbs out in opulent welcome. Red-chested robins chatted back and forth like long-lost friends.

Dash looked up from the fishing rod he was holding and smiled. At least he was enjoying himself. Perhaps her embarrassment was what entertained him. Somehow, Savannah vowed, she'd find a way of explaining the situation to her parents without complicating matters with Dash.

Holding a cold can of beer in one hand, Dash joined her, grinning as though he just learned he'd won the lottery.

"Wipe that smug look off your face," she muttered under her breath, not wanting her parents to hear. It was unlikely they would, busy as they were with the barbecue.

"You should have mentioned something earlier," Dash said, his smile brighter than ever. "I hadn't a clue you were so taken with me."

"Dash, please. I'm embarrassed enough as it is."

"But why?"

"Don't play dumb." She was fast losing her patience with him. The misunderstanding delighted him and mortified her. "I'm going to have to say something," she said, more for her own benefit than his.

"Don't. Your father might decide to barbecue hamburgers instead. It isn't every day his only daughter brings home a potential husband."

"Stop it," she whispered forcefully. "We both know the way you feel about marriage."

"I wouldn't object if you wanted to live with me."

Savannah glared at him so hard, her eyes ached with the effort.

"I was only joking." He took a swig of beer and poised the bottle in front of his lips, his look thoughtful. "Then again, maybe I wasn't."

Savannah was so furious she had to walk away. To her dismay, Dash followed her to the back of the yard, where her mother's roses were in full bloom. Glancing over her shoulder, she caught sight of her parents talking.

"You're making this situation impossible," she told him furiously.

"How's that?" His eyes fairly sparkled.

"Don't, please don't." She didn't often plead, but she did so now, struggling to keep her voice from wobbling.

Dash frowned. "What's wrong?"

She bit into her lower lip so hard, she feared she might have drawn blood. "My parents would like to see me settled down and married. They...they believe I'm like every other woman and—"

"You aren't?"

Savannah would have liked to believe his question was sincere, but similar queries from other men had all too often proved otherwise. "I'm handicapped. Men want a woman who's whole and perfect. Their egos ride on that, and I'm flawed. Defective merchandise doesn't do much for the ego.''

"Savannah..."

She pressed her hand against his chest. "Please don't say it. Spare me the speech—I've heard it all a thousand times. I've accepted the fact I'm crippled. I've accepted the fact I'll never run or jump or marry or have children."

Dash stepped back from her, his gaze pinning hers. "You're right, Savannah. You are handicapped and will be until you view yourself otherwise." Having said that, he turned and walked away.

Savannah strolled in the opposite direction, needing a few moments to compose herself before rejoining the others. She heard her mother's laughter and turned to see her father with his arms wrapped around Joyce's waist, nuzzling her neck. From a distance they looked twenty years younger. Their love was as alive now as it had been years earlier, and that was the purpose of this visit.

Her gaze scanned the yard, looking for Dash, wanting him to witness the happy exchange between her parents, but he was busy studying the fishing flies her father had left out for his inspection.

Her father's shout alerted Savannah that dinner was ready. Reluctantly she joined Dash and her parents at the round redwood picnic table. She wasn't given any choice but to share the crescent-shaped bench with him.

He was close enough that she could feel the heat radiating off his body. Close enough that she yearned to be closer yet. That was what surprised her, but more profoundly it terrified her. From the first moment she'd met Dash, Savannah suspected there was something different about him, about her reactions to him. In the beginning she attributed it to their differences of opinion, his heated argument against marriage, the challenge he represented, the promise of satisfaction if she could change his mind.

Dinner was delicious and Dash went out of his way to compliment Joyce until her mother blushed with pleasure.

"So," her father said, glancing purposefully toward Savannah and Dash, "what are your plans?"

"For what?" Dash asked.

Savannah already knew the question almost as well as she did the answer. Her father was asking about the future and she had none with Dash. This one evening was the extent of it. From here on out they would have no contact, no reason to see each other. From here on out she would go back to her life and he would return to his.

"Why don't you tell Dash how you and Mom met," Savannah suggested, interrupting her father before he could respond to Dash's question.

"Oh, Savannah," her mother protested, "that was years and years ago." She glanced toward her husband of thirty-three years and her clear eyes lit up with a love so strong, it couldn't be disguised. "But it was terribly romantic."

"You want to hear this?" Marcus's question was directed to Dash.

"By all means."

In that moment, Savannah could have kissed Dash, she was so grateful. "I was in the service," her father explained. "An Airborne Ranger. A few days before I met Joyce, I received my shipping orders and learned I was about to be stationed in Germany."

"He'd come up from California and was at Fort Lewis," her mother added.

"There's not much to tell. Two weeks before I was scheduled to leave I met Joyce at a dance."

"Daddy, you left out the best part," Savannah complained. "It wasn't like the band was playing a number you enjoyed and you needed a partner."

Her father chuckled. "You're right about that. I'd gone to the dance with a couple of buddies of mine. The evening hadn't been going well."

"As I remember, you'd been stood up," Savannah inserted, eager to get on to the details of their romance.

"No, dear," her mother intervened, picking up the story line, "that was me. As you can imagine I was in no mood to be at any social function. The only reason I decided to go was to be sure Lenny Walton knew I hadn't sat home and mooned over him, but in reality I was at the dance mooning over him."

"I wasn't particularly keen on being at this dance, either," Marcus added. "I thought, mistakenly, that we were going to play pool at a local hall. I never have been much of a dancer, but my buddies were. They disappeared onto the dance floor almost immediately. Consequently I was bored and wandered around the hall for a while. I kept looking at my watch, eager to be on my way."

"As you can imagine, I wasn't dancing much myself," Joyce added.

"Then it happened." Savannah pressed her palms together and leaned forward. "This is my favorite part," she told Dash.

"What is?" Dash frowned.

"Shh." She silenced him.

"I saw Joyce." Her father's voice dipped slightly at the memory. "When I first caught sight of her, something caught in my chest. I thought for a moment I might be having a reaction to the shots we'd been given earlier in the day. I swear I'd never seen a more beautiful woman in my life. She wore this white dress and she looked like one of heaven's own angels standing there. For a moment I was convinced she was." Her father reached for her mother's hand.

"I saw Marcus at that precise moment, as well," Joyce whispered. "My friends were chatting on around me and their voices faded until the only sound I heard was the pounding of my own heart. I don't remember walking toward him and yet I must have, because when I looked up Marcus was standing there."

"The funny part is, I don't remember moving, either."

Savannah propped her elbows against the table, her dinner forgotten. This was the best part of the story; it never failed to move her, although she'd heard it dozens of times over the years.

"We danced," her mother continued.

"All night."

"We didn't say a word. I think we must have been afraid the other would vanish if we spoke."

"While we were on the dance floor I kept pinching myself to be sure this was real, that Joyce was real. It was like we were both in a wild, romantic dream. These sort of things only happen in the movies.

"When the music stopped, I looked around and realized my buddies were gone. It didn't matter. Nothing mattered but Joyce."

"Oh, Dad, I never tire of hearing this story."

Joyce smiled dreamily as if she, too, were eager to relive the events of that night. "As we were walking out of the hall, I kept thinking I was never going to see Marcus again. I knew he was in the army—his haircut was a dead giveaway. I was well aware my parents didn't want me dating anyone in the military, and up until then I'd abided by their wishes."

"I was afraid I wasn't going to be able to see her again," Savannah's father continued. "Joyce gave me her name and phone number and then hurried to catch up with her ride home."

"I didn't sleep at all that night, convinced I'd imagined everything."

"I couldn't sleep, either," Marcus confessed. "Here I was with my shipping orders in my hip pocket—this was not the time to get involved with a woman."

"I'm pleased you changed your mind," Dash said, studying Savannah.

"To tell you the truth, I don't think I had much of a choice. It was as if our relationship was pre-ordained from above. By the end of the following week, I knew Joyce was the woman I would eventually marry. I also was convinced I would love her all my life, and both have held true."

"Did you leave for Germany?"

"Of course. I had no choice. We wrote back and forth for two long years and then were married three months after I was discharged. There was never another woman for me after I met Joyce."

"There was never another man for me," her mother added.

Savannah tossed Dash a triumphant look and was disappointed to realize he wasn't looking her way.

"It's a romantic story." He was gracious enough to admit that much.

"Apparently some of that romance rubbed off on Savannah." Her father's eyes were proud as he looked to her. "This wedding business of hers is thriving."

"So it seems." Some of the enthusiasm diminished from Dash's voice. He was apparently thinking of his sister, and Savannah's role in her wedding plans.

"Eat, before your dinner gets cold," Joyce instructed, waving her steak knife in their direction.

"How long did you say you've been married?" Dash asked, dragging his knife over the meat.

"Thirty-three years," her father told him.

"And it's been smooth sailing through all that time?"

Savannah wanted to pound her fist against the table and announce that this cross-examination was unnecessary.

Marcus laughed. "Smooth sailing? Oh, hardly. Joyce and I've had our ups and downs over the years like most couples. If there's anything special about our marriage, it's been our commitment to one another."

Savannah cleared her throat, wanting to gloat. Once more Dash ignored her.

"You've never once entertained the idea of divorce?" he pressed.

This line of questioning was unfair. She hadn't had the opportunity to challenge his clients about their divorces, not that she would have wanted to. Every case had saddened and depressed her.

"You see, once a couple introduces the subject of divorce, the doors of communication and problem solving aren't nearly as flexible," Marcus said. "There's always that out, always the possibility."

Joyce nodded. "If there was any one key to the success of our marriage, it's been that we've refused to consider divorce an option. That's not to say I haven't thought of it a time or two."

"We're only human," her father agreed with a swift shake of his head. "I'll admit I've entertained the notion a time or two myself."

No! It wasn't true. Savannah didn't believe it. "But never seriously?" she felt obliged to ask.

Marcus looked her way and offered her a sympathetic smile, as if aware of their wager. "Your mother and I love each other, and neither of us could say we're sorry we stuck it out through the hard times, but yes, sweetheart, there were those odd times when I didn't know if our marriage would survive."

Her parents' timing was incredible. If they were going to be brutally honest, why, oh, why did it have to be now? In all the years Savannah was growing up she'd never once heard the word *divorce* mentioned. She wasn't even aware her parents argued. In her eyes their marriage was perfect, always had been and always would be. Now this.

Savannah dared not look at Dash, certain he was taking delight in flaunting his victory in her face.

"So, what do you think of our little girl?" Marcus asked, when he'd finished his dinner. He placed his hands on his stomach and studied Dash.

"Dad, please, you're embarrassing me."

"Why?"

"My guess is Savannah would prefer we didn't give her friend the third degree, dear," Joyce suggested.

It was all Savannah could do not to kiss her mother's cheek. She stood, eager to disentangle herself from this knot-producing conversation. "I'll help you with the dishes, Mom,'' she said as if suggesting a shopping trip to the mall.

Dash's mood had improved considerably after meeting Savannah's parents. It was apparent matters weren't going the way she'd planned. Twice now, during dinner, it was all he could manage not to laugh out loud. Clearly she was looking for them to paint a rosy picture of their idyllic lives together, convince him of the error of his ways.

The project had all but backfired in her face. Rarely had he seen anyone look more shocked than when her parents announced divorce was something they'd each contemplated at one point or another in their long-term marriage.

The men cleared the picnic table and the two women shooed them out of the kitchen. Dash was grateful, since he had several questions he longed to ask Marcus about Savannah.

The two wandered back outside. Dash was helping Marcus gather up his fishing gear when Savannah's father spoke.

"I didn't mean to pry earlier," he said casually, lugging his fishing rod and box of flies into the garage. A motor home was parked alongside of the building. Although it was an older model, it looked as good as new.

"You don't need to worry about offending me," Dash assured him.

"I wasn't worried about you. Savannah gave me 'the look' while we were eating. I don't know how much experience you have with women, young man, but take my advice, when you see 'the look,' shut up.

No matter what it is you're discussing, if you value your life, don't say another word.''

Dash chuckled. "I'll keep that in mind."

"Savannah's got the same look as her mother. If you continue dating her, you'll recognize it soon enough. You are going to continue seeing my daughter, aren't you?"

"You wouldn't object?"

"Heavens, no. If you don't mind me being curious, tell me, what do you think of my little girl?"

Dash didn't mince words. "She's the most incredibly stubborn woman I've ever met."

Marcus nodded and poised his prize fishing rod against the wall. "She gets that from her mother, as well." He turned around to face Dash, hands on his hips. "Does her limp bother you?" he asked point-blank.

"Yes and no." Dash wouldn't discredit her father with a half-truth. "It bothers me because she's so conscious of it herself."

Marcus's chest swelled as he exhaled. "That she is."

"How'd it happen?" Curiosity got the better of him, although he'd prefer to hear the explanation from Savannah.

Her father walked to the back of the garage where a youngster's mangled bicycle was stored. "It makes it sound simple to say she was hit by a car. This was what was left of her bicycle. I've kept it all these years as a reminder of how far she's come."

"Dear God," Dash breathed when he viewed the mangled frame and guessed the full extent of the damage done to the youngster riding it. "How'd she ever survive?"

"I'm not being facetious when I say sheer nerve. Anyone else with less fortitude would have willed death. She was in the hospital for months, and that was only the beginning. The doctors first told us she'd never walk again, and for the first year we believed it was true.

"Even now the pain is with her. Some days it's better than others. Climate seems to affect it somewhat. Her limp is more pronounced when she's overly tired." Marcus replaced the bicycle and turned to Dash. "It isn't every man who recognizes Savannah's strength. You haven't asked for my advice, so forgive me for being so free to offer it."

"Please."

"My daughter's a special woman, but she's a prickly thing when it comes to men and relationships. Somehow she's got it in her head that no man will ever want her."

"I'm sure that's not true."

"It's true, simply because Savannah believes it is," Marcus corrected. "It will take a rare man to overpower her defenses. I'm not saying you're that man. I'm not even saying you should try."

"You seemed to think otherwise earlier. Wasn't it you who assumed I should marry your daughter?"

"I said that to get a rise out of Savannah, and by heaven, it worked." Marcus rubbed the side of his jaw, his eyes twinkling with delight.

"We've only just met." Dash felt he had to offer some explanation, although he wasn't sure why.

"I know." He slapped Dash affectionately across the back and together the two of them left the garage. By the time they returned to the house, the dinner dishes had been washed and put away.

Savannah's mother had filled several containers of leftovers and packed them into a brown bag. Apparently she felt they'd both be overcome with hunger on the way home.

Savannah retrieved her purse while her mother offered Dash instructions on how to properly warm up the leftovers. Attempting brain surgery sounded simpler. As it happened, Dash caught a glimpse of Marcus from the corner of his eye and nearly burst out laughing. The older man had placed his hands over his ears, and was slowing shaking his head.

"I like the coyote, Mom," Savannah said, running her hand over the pink plaster animal. "Are you and Dad going to Arizona this winter?"

Dash felt static electricity hit the airwaves.

"We haven't decided, but I doubt that we will this year," Joyce answered.

"Why not?" Savannah asked in what sounded like an open-ended challenge. "You love it there. More and more of your friends are becoming snowbirds. It doesn't make sense for you to waste your winters here in the cold and damp when you can be with your friends, soaking up the sunshine."

"Sweetheart, we've got a long time to make that decision," Marcus reminded her. "It's barely summer."

"What was that all about?" Dash asked once they were in his car.

It was rare to see Savannah look vulnerable but she did so now. He wasn't any expert when it came to dealing with women. His sister was evidence of that, and every other female he'd ever had contact with, for that matter. It looked as though gutsy Savannah was about to burst into tears.

"It's nothing," she said, her voice so low it was almost nonexistent. Her head was turned away from him and she was staring out the side window.

"Tell me," he insisted as he reached the freeway's on ramp. He increased the car's speed.

Savannah clenched her hands together. "They won't leave because of me." Again her voice was as thin as a silk thread. "They seem to think I need a baby-sitter, that it's their duty to watch after me."

"Are you sure you're not being overly sensitive?"

"I'm sure. Mom and Dad love to travel and now that Dad's retired they should be doing much more of it."

"They have the motor home."

"They seldom use it. Day trips, a drive to the ocean once or twice a year, and that's about it. Dad would love to explore the East Coast in the autumn, but I doubt that he ever will."

"Why not?"

"They're afraid something will happen to me."

"It sounds like they're being overprotective."

"They are," Savannah cried. "But I can't force them to go, and they won't listen to me."

There was more to this story than what was apparent. "What's the real reason, Savannah?" He made his words as coaxing as he could, not wanting to pressure her into telling him something she'd later regret.

"They blame themselves for the accident," she whispered. "They were leaving for a weekend trip that day and I was to stay with a baby-sitter. I'd wanted to go with them and when they said I couldn't, I got upset. In order to appease me, Dad said I could ride my bicycle instead. Up until that time he'd always gone with me."

Dash chanced a look at her and noted her eyes were closed and her body was rigid with tension.

"And so they punish themselves," she continued in halting tones, "thinking if they sacrifice their lives for me, it will absolve them from their guilt. Instead it increases mine."

"Yours?"

"Do you mind if we don't discuss this subject?" she asked, sounding physically tired and emotionally beaten.

The silence that followed rattled around in the car like shoes in the clothes dryer. It was broken by Savannah's sigh of defeat.

"When would you like me to start cooking your dinners?" she asked as they neared her shop.

"You're conceding?" Keeping the shock out of his voice was impossible. "Just like that, without so much as an argument? You must be more tired than I realized."

His comments produced a sad smile.

"So you're willing to admit marriage is a thing of the past and has no part in this day and age?" he pressed.

"Never!" She rallied a bit at that.

"That's what I thought."

"Are you ready to admit love can last a lifetime when nourished and respected?" she asked.

Dash frowned, his thoughts confused. "I'll grant there are exceptions to every rule and your parents are clearly that. Unfortunately, the love they share doesn't exist between most married couples.

"It'd be easy to tell you I like my macaroni and cheese extra cheesy," he went on to say, "but I have a feeling that you'll change your mind in the morning and demand a rematch.''

Savannah smiled and pressed the side of her head against the car window.

''You're exhausted, and if I graciously accepted your defeat, you'd never forgive me.''

''What do you suggest, then?''

''A draw.'' He pulled into the alley behind the shop to where Savannah had parked her car. ''Let's call it square. I said what I wanted to say and you proved what you wanted to prove. There's no need to go back to the beginning and start again because neither of us is going to make progress with the other. We're both too strongheaded for that.''

''We should have recognized that sooner,'' Savannah said, eyes closed.

She was so damn delectable, Dash had to force himself to look away.

''It's very gentlemanly of you not to accept my defeat.''

''Not really.''

Her eyes slowly opened and she rotated her head so she could look him in the eyes. ''Why not?''

''Because I'm about to incur your wrath.''

''Really? How's that?''

He smiled. It had been so damn long since he'd looked more forward to anything. ''Because, my dear wedding coordinator, I'm about to kiss you senseless.''

Chapter Four

"You're going to kiss me?" Savannah had been exhausted seconds earlier, but Dash's words produced a shot of adrenaline that bolted her upright.

"I most certainly am," Dash said, parking his car behind her own vehicle in the dark alley. "Don't look so damned frightened. The fact is, you might even enjoy this."

That was what terrified Savannah most. If ever there was a man whose touch she yearned for, it was Dash. If ever there was a man she longed to hold her, it was Dash.

He bent his head toward hers and what resistance she'd managed to amass died a sudden death as he pressed his chin to her temple and simply held her against him. If he'd been rough or demanding or anything else but gentle, she might have had a chance at resisting him. A sigh rumbled through her breast and with heedless curiosity she lifted her hand to his face, her fingertips grazing the stubborn side of his jaw. Her touch, light and sweet, seemed to go through him like an electrical shock because he groaned and, as she tilted back her head, his mouth sought hers.

Her lips parted instinctively in need and welcome and he drew her possessively against him, his arms surrounding her. Savannah reached for him, too, raising her flattened palms upward until she gripped his collar with tight fists, as if she needed something to center her. The action must have been instinctive because in the next moment, Dash's tongue invaded her mouth, swirling about, stroking hers.

At the blast of unexpected sensation, Savannah buckled against him and whimpered, all the while clinging to him. The kiss continued, gaining in intensity and fervor until Savannah felt certain her heart would pound straight through her chest.

She was hot, hotter than she could ever remember being, as if she'd lain too long in the scorching sun. Suddenly she was cool, the rush of air against her bare skin coming as a shock. It wasn't until then that she realized Dash had lifted her sweater and freed her breasts. The cool night air felt like an Arctic breeze against her heated skin. Dash's hands moved over her, caressing, kneading the heaviness of her full breasts, acquainting himself with their shape.

Savannah felt herself sinking into a maze of sensual awareness she'd once only speculated was real. One of them moaned, but she wasn't sure if it was Dash or herself. Hot sensation enveloped her, freeing her inhibitions. When Dash dragged his mouth from hers, she groaned, not wanting him to stop. Her disappointment was only momentary as his moist lips sought a nipple. His tongue washed over the throbbing hardness with warm, gentle strokes as his hands bunched the weight of her breasts together. He paid equal attention to both nipples, sucking long and slow at each pearled bead.

Clasping his head, Savannah held him against her, her eyes closed to a world of sensual pleasure.

"Savannah." Her name was a tortured groan. His breathing, heavy and hard, came in soft bursts as he struggled to regain control. Savannah was struggling, too. Slowly, thoughtfully, she opened her eyes. Her fingers were rammed deep into his thick head of hair; she sighed and relaxed her punishing hold.

Dash lifted his head and captured her face between his hands, his gaze delving into hers. "I didn't mean for that to happen."

An apology. She should have expected it, should have been prepared for it. But she wasn't.

He seemed to be waiting for her to respond so she gave him the best she had to offer, which was a weak, ambiguous smile, and she lowered her gaze, not wanting him to guess how strong her reaction had been.

He pressed his forehead to hers and chuckled softly. "You're a surprise a minute."

"What . . . do you mean?" she whispered.

He dropped a glancing kiss against the side of her face. "Who would have believed someone so small would reveal such passion? You went straight to my head." As he was speaking, he righted her clothes. Savannah was grateful for the help; she doubted that she would have been able to rearrange her clothing had she tried to do so on her own.

"In other words, you didn't expect a cripple to experience sensual pleasure?" she demanded righteously. "It might surprise you to know I'm still a woman."

"What?" Dash said. The edge of his voice would have been cutting if it hadn't been for the shock that leaked into the lone word.

"You heard me," she said, frantically searching for her purse and the bag of leftovers her mother had insisted she take home with her.

"Stop," he demanded, gripping her upper arms. "Don't use insults to ruin something that was both beautiful and spontaneous."

"I wasn't the one issuing—"

She wasn't allowed to finish. His hands tightened around her upper arms and he hauled her toward him until his mouth smothered hers. Her resistance was taken as she was caught, once again, in the powerful persuasion of his kisses.

He exhaled sharply when he finished. "Your leg has nothing to do with this. Nothing. Do you understand?"

"Why were you so surprised, then?" she demanded, struggling to keep her indignation alive. It was almost impossible to do so when she was in his arms.

His answer took a long time coming. "I don't know."

"That's what I thought." She broke away and gathered her purse against her like a protective shield. "We've agreed to disagree on the issue of love and marriage, isn't that correct?"

"Yes," he said with no emotion.

"Then I don't see any reason for us to continue our debate. It's been a pleasure meeting you, Mr. Davenport. Goodbye." Having said that much, she jerked open the car door and nearly toppled backward. She caught herself in the nick of time before tumbling headfirst into the alleyway.

"Savannah, for the love of heaven, will you—"

"Please, just leave me alone," she said, furious now with herself for making such a dramatic exit and with him for reasons as yet unclear.

Because he made her feel, she guessed, when she was home and safe. He made her feel as if she was whole and without flaws. As if she was an attractive, desirable woman. Savannah blamed Dash for this and the anger simmered in her blood long after she readied for bed.

Neatly folding her bedspread at the foot of her mattress, Savannah stood, seething, tears so close to the surface that she was forced to take in deep, even breaths to keep them at bay. She wasn't like other women, and never would be. Dash had done her a grave disservice to pretend otherwise. That was what she found so painful.

In the morning, after she'd downed her first cup of coffee, Savannah felt better. She was determined to put the incident and the man out of her mind. There was no reason for them to see each other again, no reason for them to continue with this farce. Not that Dash would want to see her, especially after the idiotic way she'd behaved, climbing out of his car as if escaping a murderer.

As so often was the case of late, Savannah was wrong. Dash was waiting on the sidewalk in front of her shop, carrying a white bag, when she arrived for work.

"Another peace offering?" she asked, when she unlocked the front door and opened it for him.

"Something like that." He handed her a latte, then walked across the showroom and sat on the corner of her desk. He dangled one leg as if he had every right to make himself comfortable in her place of business.

Savannah had yet to recover from seeing him again so soon. She wasn't ready emotionally or physically for another confrontation. "What can I do for you?" she asked stiffly, setting the hot milk and coffee aside. She sat down and leaned back in the swivel chair, hoping she looked relaxed, knowing she didn't.

"I've come to answer your question," he said, leg swinging as he pried loose the lid of his latte. He was so blasé about everything, as if the intensity of their foreplay was a common thing for him. As if she was one in a long line of near conquests. "You wanted to know what was different last night and I'm here to tell you."

This was the last thing Savannah anticipated. She glanced pointedly at her watch. "Is this going to take long? I've got an appointment in ten minutes."

"I'll be out of here before your client arrives."

"Good." She crossed her arms over her chest, having a problem holding on to her patience. Their kisses embarrassed her now. She was determined to push it out of her mind and forget him. It'd been crazy to place a wager with him. It'd been fun, but it'd been sheer folly. The best she could do was to forget she'd ever met the man. Dash, however, seemed determined not to let that happen.

"Well?" she pressed when he didn't immediately speak his piece.

"A woman doesn't generally go to my head the way you did," he said, and unyielding pride echoed in his voice. "When I make love to a woman I'm the one in control."

"We weren't making love," she said heatedly, heat flushing her cheeks with instant color. Her fingers bit into the soft flesh of her arms as she struggled to keep the embarrassment to herself.

"What the hell do you call it, then?"

"Kissing."

"In the beginning, but it would have developed into something a whole lot more complicated if we hadn't been in my car. The last time I made love in the back seat of a car, I was—"

"This may come as a surprise to you, but I have no interest in listening to your sexual exploits," she interjected.

"Fine," he snapped.

"Besides, we were nowhere near making love."

Dash's responding snort sent ripples of outrage through Savannah. "You overestimate your appeal, Mr. Davenport."

Dash laughed outright this time. "Somehow or other, I thought you'd say as much. I was hoping you'd be a bit more honest, but then, I've found truth an uncommon trait with most women."

The bell above her door chimed just then, as her appointment strolled into the shop. Savannah was so grateful to have this uncomfortable conversation interrupted, it was all she could do not to hug her client.

"I'd love to continue this debate," she lied. Blatantly. "But as you can see, I have a customer."

"Perhaps another time," Dash suggested.

She hesitated. "Perhaps."

He snickered disdainfully as he stood and sipped from the thick cardboard cup. "As I said, women seem to have the damnedest time dealing with the truth."

Savannah pretended not to hear him as she walked toward her customer, a warm welcoming smile planted on her face. "Good morning, Mrs. Larson. I see you're right on time."

Dash said nothing as he sauntered past her and out the door. Not until he was out of sight did Savannah relax her guard. He claimed she went to his head. What he didn't know was that his effect upon her was startlingly similar. Then again, perhaps he did know.

Damn, but the woman irritated him. No, Dash decided as he hit the sidewalk, his stride clipped and fast paced, she more than irritated him. Savannah Charles incensed him. He didn't understand this oppressive need he experienced to talk to her, to explain, to hear her thoughts. He'd wakened wishing matters hadn't ended so abruptly between them, wishing he'd known what to say to convince her of his sincerity. Morning felt like a second chance.

In retrospect, he suspected he was looking for help himself in sorting through the powerful play of emotions that had evolved with their embrace. Instead, Savannah had taken delight in pointing out the error of his ways, in claiming he'd miscalculated her reaction. The hell he had. She was as hot as he was.

He should have realized she was as much at a loss as he to put meaning into their explosive response to each other. Dash wasn't into game playing. If Savannah wanted to believe otherwise, he'd let her, without a qualm and without regrets.

Dash arrived at his office several minutes later than normal. As he walked past his secretary's desk, she handed him several telephone messages. He was due in court within twenty minutes, and wouldn't have time to return any calls until early afternoon. Shuffling through the slips, he stopped at the third one as surprise gripped hold of him.

Susan.

His sister had telephoned him. With little forethought he set his briefcase aside and reached for the phone, punching out the number listed.

"Susan, it's Dash," he said when she answered the phone. If he hadn't been so damn eager to talk to her, he might have mulled over the reason for her call. Something must have happened, otherwise she wouldn't have swallowed her pride to contact him.

"Hello, Dash."

He waited several moments in vain for her to explain herself. "You called me?"

"Yes," she said abruptly, as if the word had been being jerked from her. "I wanted to apologize for hanging up on you the other day. It was rude and unnecessary. Kurt and I had a...discussion about it and he said I owed you an apology."

"Kurt's got a good head on his shoulders," he said, thinking his sister would laugh and the tension between them would ease. It didn't.

"I thought about what he had to say and Kurt's right. I'm sorry for the way I reacted."

"I'm sorry, too," Dash admitted. "I shouldn't have checked up on you behind your back." If she could be so generous with her forgiveness, then so could he. After all, Susan was his little sister. He had her best interests at heart, although she wouldn't fully appreciate his concern until later in life, when she was responsible for children of her own. He wasn't Susan's father, but he was her nearest male relative. Although she was twenty-one, she continued to need his guidance and direction.

"I was thinking we might have lunch together some afternoon," she ventured, and the way her voice wobbled revealed how uneasy she was in making the suggestion.

Dash had missed their lunch get-togethers. "That sounds like a good idea to me. How about Thursday?"

"Same place as always?"

There was a Mexican restaurant that was their favorite, on a steep side street not far from the King County courthouse. They'd made a point of meeting there for lunch at least once a month for the past several years. The waitresses were familiar enough to greet them by name.

"All right. I'll see you Thursday at noon."

"Great."

Grinning, Dash replaced the receiver.

He looked forward to this luncheon date with his sister the way a kid anticipates the arrival of the Easter bunny. They'd both said and done things they regretted. Dash hadn't changed his mind about his sister marrying Kurt Caldwell. Kurt was decent enough, intelligent, hardworking and sincere, but they were both much too young to be thinking about marriage. From

Susan's reaction, she wasn't likely to heed his advice. He hated to think of her making the same mistakes he had, but there didn't seem to be any help for it. He might as well mend the bridges of communication before they became irreparable.

"Is something wrong?" Susan asked Savannah as they went over the details for the wedding. It bothered her how careful Susan and Kurt had to be with their money. She admired the couple's discipline. Each decision had been painstaking.

"I'm sorry." Savannah's mind clearly wasn't on the subject at hand. It had taken a sharp turn in another direction the moment Susan had arrived for their appointment. Until then Savannah hadn't recognized the striking resemblance between brother and sister. Susan and Dash shared the same eye and hair color, true, but they were alike in other ways, as well. The way Susan smiled and her easy laugh were Dash's trademarks.

Savannah had worked hard to push all thoughts of Dash from her mind. Naively, she felt she'd succeeded, until Susan had stepped into the shop.

Savannah didn't know what it was about this hardheaded cynic that attracted her so strongly. It plagued her no end that he would be the one to ignite the spark of her sensual nature. There was no future for them. Not when their views on love and marriage diametrically opposed each other.

"Savannah," Susan asked, "are you feeling all right?"

"Of course. I'm sorry, my thoughts seem to be a thousand miles away."

"I noticed," Susan said with a subtle laugh.

Her mood certainly seemed to have lifted since their previous meeting, Savannah noticed, wishing she could say the same. Dash hadn't contacted her since their last disastrous confrontation a few days earlier. Not that she expected he would.

Susan stepped into the wedding dress and lifted her hair at the back so Savannah could connect the long row of pearl buttons.

"I'm having lunch with Dash on Thursday," Susan announced unexpectedly.

"I'm pleased to hear you two have patched your differences."

Susan's shoulders moved up and down with a reflective sigh. "We haven't exactly—at least, not yet. I called him to apologize for hanging up the phone on him. He must have been eager to talk to me because his secretary told me he was due in court that morning and I shouldn't expect to hear from him until later that afternoon. He phoned back no more than five minutes later."

"He loves you very much." Savannah's fingers expertly fastened the pearls around the silk loops. Dash had proved he was capable of caring deeply for another human being, yet he staunchly denied the healing power of love into his own life.

Perhaps you're doing the same thing.

The thought came at her like the burning flash from a laser gun, too fast to avoid, and too painful to ignore. It sliced through the thick skin of her dignity and her pride. Savannah shook her head to chase away the doubts. It was ridiculous. She'd purposely chosen a career that was steeped in love and romance. To suggest she was blocking the emotion from her own life was ludicrous. Yet the accusation was shouted back to her like an echo, repeating itself over and over, waning with each sequence until it rang hollow and empty in a dark alcove in her mind.

"Savannah?"

"I'm finished," she said quickly. Startled, she stepped back.

Susan dropped her arms and shook her hair free before slowly turning around to face Savannah. "Well?" she asked breathlessly. "What do you think?"

Although her mind was preoccupied with a series of haunting doubts, Savannah couldn't help admiring how beautiful Dash's sister looked in the bridal gown. "Oh, Susan, you're lovely."

The young woman viewed herself in the mirror, staring at her reflection for several moments as if she wasn't sure she could believe what she was seeing.

"I'm going to ask Dash to attend the wedding when we have lunch," she announced. Then, biting into her lower lip, she added, "I'm praying he'll agree to that much."

"He should." Savannah didn't want to build up Susan's expectations. She honestly couldn't predict what Dash would say; she only knew what she thought he should do.

"He sounded so pleased to hear from me," Susan went on to say.

"I'm sure he was." They stood next to each other in front of the mirror. Neither seemed inclined to move. Savannah couldn't speak for Susan, but for her part, the mirror grounded her in the reality of her situation. Her reflection revealed her scarred and twisted leg, a not-so-gentle reminder of her deficiency.

"Let me know what Dash says," Savannah said impulsively just before Susan left the shop.

"I will." Susan's eyes revealed a childlike quality as she turned and walked away.

Savannah sat at her desk and wrote down the pertinent facts she needed to remember about the wedding gown she was ordering for Susan, but as her hand moved the pen across the paper, her thoughts weren't on the dress measurements. Instead they drifted on a one-way freeway straight to Dash. If nothing else, he had given her pause to think over her life and face up to a few uncomfortable truths. That wasn't a bad day's work for a skeptical divorce attorney. It was unfortunate he'd never realize the impact he'd had on her.

Dash was waiting in the booth, anxiously glancing at his watch every fifteen seconds, convinced Susan wasn't going to show, when she strolled into the restaurant. A smile lit up her face when she found him. It was almost as if they'd never disagreed, and she was a kid again coming to her big brother for advice.

"I'm sorry I'm late," she said, slipping into the vinyl seat across the table from him. "I'm starved," she announced, reaching for a salted chip and weighing it down with a thick glob of spicy salsa.

"It's good to see you," Dash ventured, taking the first step toward reconciliation. He'd missed Susan, although he wasn't keen on admitting as much, at least, not so soon.

"I've missed you, too. It doesn't feel right for us to fight, does it?"

"Not at all."

"You're the only real family I have."

"I feel the same way. We've both made mistakes and we should learn from them." He made a point of not casting blame. It wouldn't do any good.

The waitress delivered their menus. Dash didn't recognize the young Hispanic woman, which caused him to consider just how long it'd been since he'd last had lunch with Susan. Frowning, he realized she'd been the one to approach him about a reconciliation, when as the older, more mature adult, he should have been working toward that end himself.

"I brought you something," Susan said, setting her handbag on top of the table. She rooted through one side until she found what she was looking for. Taking the envelope from her purse, she handed it to him, her gaze studying him.

Dash accepted the envelope, peeled it open and pulled out a handcrafted wedding invitation, written on antique white parchment paper in gold letters. He didn't realize his sister knew calligraphy. Although it was obviously handmade, the effort was competent and appealing to the eye.

"I wrote it out myself," Susan said eagerly. "Savannah was the one who suggested Kurt and I would save money by making our own wedding invitations. It's much more personal this way, don't you think?"

"They're very nice."

"The gold ink on the parchment paper was Kurt's idea. Savannah gave me a book on calligraphy and I've been practicing every afternoon."

He wondered how many more times his sister would find an excuse to drag the wedding coordinator's name into their conversation. Each time Susan mentioned Savannah it brought up unwelcome memories of their few short times together. Memories Dash would rather forget.

"Do you like it?" Susan asked eagerly. She seemed to be waiting for something more.

"You did a beautiful job."

"I'm really pleased you think so."

Susan was grinning under the warmth of his approval.

The waitress returned and they placed their order, although neither of them had looked at the menu. "We're certainly creatures of habit, aren't we?" his sister teased.

"So," he said, relaxing against the high booth back, "how are the wedding plans going?"

"Very well, thanks to Savannah." She folded her hands on top of the table, flexing her long nails against each other, studying him, waiting.

Dash read over the invitation a second time and realized that it had been personally written out to him. So this was the purpose of her phone call, the purpose of this lunch. She was asking him if he'd attend her wedding, knowing that he strongly disapproved.

"I don't expect you to change your mind about me marrying Kurt," Susan said anxiously, rushing the words together in her eagerness to have them said. "But it would mean the world to me if you'd attend the ceremony. There won't be a lot of people there. Just a few friends and Kurt's immediate family. That's all we can afford. Savannah's been wonderful, showing us how to get the most out of our limited budget. Will you come to my wedding, Dash?"

Dash knew when he was facing a losing battle. Susan would marry Kurt with or without his approval. His kid sister was determined to do this her way. He'd done his best to talk some sense into her, but to no avail. He'd made the mistake of threatening her, and fool that he was, she'd called his bluff. The past several weeks had been miserable for them both.

"I'll come."

"Oh, Dash, thank you." Tears brimmed and spilled over her lashes. She reached for her paper napkin, holding it beneath each eye in turn. "I can't begin to tell you how much this means to me."

"I know." Damn, he felt like crying himself, but for none of the same reasons. He didn't want to see his sister hurt and that was inevitable once she was married. "I still don't approve of your marrying so young, but I can't stop you."

"Dash, you keep forgetting, I'm over twenty-one. You make me sound like a baby."

He sighed expressively. That was the way he saw her, as his baby sister. It was difficult to think of her married, with a family of her own, when it only seemed a few years back when she was in diapers.

"You'll like Kurt once you get to know him better," she said excitedly, wiping the moisture from her cheek. "Look at what you've done to me," she muttered. Her mascara streaked her face in inky rows.

His hand reached for hers and he squeezed her fingers. "We'll get through this yet, kid," he joked.

Dash suspected, in the days that followed, that it was natural to feel good about making his sister so happy. All he'd been willing to do was attend the ceremony. He hadn't figured out what was going to keep him in his seat when the minister asked anyone who opposed the union to speak now or forever hold their peace. Attending the ceremony itself, regardless of his personal feelings toward marriage, was the least he could do for causing the rift between them.

The card from Savannah that arrived at his office took him by surprise. He stared at the return address listed on the envelope for several moments before turning it over and opening it with eager fingers. Her message was straightforward enough: "Thank you."

Her delicate, slanted signature was penned below.

Dash held the card for several minutes before slapping it down on his desk top. The damn fool woman was driving him to distraction.

He left the office almost immediately, shocking his secretary, who rushed after him, needing to know what she was supposed to do about his next appointment. Dash suggested she entertain him with some law journals and coffee. He promised to be back in fifteen minutes.

Luckily he found a parking spot on the street. Climbing out of his car, he strolled purposely toward the bridal shop. Savannah was sitting at her desk intent on her task. When she glanced up and saw it was him, she froze.

"I got your card," he said stiffly.

"I... It made Susan so happy to know you'd attend her wedding. I wanted to thank you," she offered, her eyes following his every movement.

He marched to her desk, not understanding even now what force had driven him to her. "How many guests is she inviting?"

"I... believe the number's around sixty."

"Change that," he instructed harshly. "We're going to be inviting three hundred or more. I'll have the list to you in the morning."

"Susan and Kurt can't afford..."

"They won't be paying for it. I will. I want the best for my sister, understand. No more of these hand-written invitations. We'll have a sit-down dinner, a dance with a ten-piece orchestra, real flowers and a designer wedding dress. Have you got that?" He motioned toward her pen, thinking she'd best write it down.

Savannah looked as if she hadn't heard him. "Does Susan know about all this?"

"Not yet."

"Don't you think you should clear all this with her first?"

"It might be too soon, because a good deal of this hinges on one thing."

Savannah frowned. "What's that?"

"If you'll agree to attend the wedding as my date."

Chapter Five

"**Y**our date," Savannah repeated as she leapt to her feet. No easy task when one leg was as unsteady as her own. She didn't often forget that, but she did now in her incredulity. "That's emotional blackmail," she cried, before slumping back into her chair.

"You're damn right it is," Dash agreed, leaning forward and pressing his hands against the edge of her oak desk. His face was scant inches from her own, and his eyes cut straight through her defenses. "It's what you expect of me, isn't it?" he demanded. "Being I'm so despicable."

"I never said that."

"Maybe not," he agreed, "but you accused me of using you."

"I . . . didn't!" she snapped, then thinking perhaps she had, she blinked several times in an effort to remember the gist of their conversation that night. She'd been shaken to the core of her being by his kiss, and then he'd apologized as if he'd never meant for it to happen, and perhaps worse, that he wished it hadn't.

A slow, leisurely smile replaced Dash's dark scowl. "That's what I thought," he said as he lifted his hand and brushed a strand of hair from her forehead. His fingertips lingered at her face. "I wish I knew what the hell's happening to us."

"Nothing's happening," Savannah insisted, but her voice lacked conviction even to her own ears. She was fighting the powerful attraction she felt for him for all she was worth, which at the moment wasn't much. "You aren't really going to blackmail me, are you?"

His fingertips gently traced the outline of her face, pausing at her chin and tilting it upward. "Do you agree to attend the wedding with me?"

"Yes, only..."

"Then you should know I had no intention of following through with my threat. Susan can have the wedding of her dreams."

Savannah stood, awkwardly placing her weight on her injured leg. "I'm sure there are far more suitable dates for you," she said crisply, praying he'd listen to reason.

"I want you."

He made this so damn difficult. "Why me?" she asked, her vulnerability punctuating the single word. By his own admission, there were any number of other women who would jump at the chance to date him. Why had he insisted upon singling out her? It made no sense. Little did any more, she discovered.

Dash frowned as if he wasn't sure himself, which lent credence to Savannah's revolving doubts. "I don't know. As for this wedding business, it seemed to me I could be wrong. It doesn't happen often, but I have been known to make an error in judgment now and again. Susan's my only sister—hell, she's the only family I've got. I don't want there to be any regrets between us. Your card helped, too, and the way I see it, if I'm going to sit through a wedding, I'm not going to suffer alone. I want you there with me." His gaze narrowed as if he didn't understand it even now.

"Then I suggest you ask someone who'd appreciate the invitation," she said defiantly, straightening her shoulders.

"I want to be with you," he insisted softly, his eyes revealing his confusion. "The hell if I know why. You're stubborn, defensive and argumentative."

"One would think you'd rather wrestle a rattlesnake than date me."

"One would think," he agreed, grinning boyishly, "but if that's the case, why do I find myself listening for the sound of your voice? Why do I look forward to spending time with you?"

"I . . . wouldn't know." Except that she found herself facing the same problem. Dash was never far from her thoughts; she hadn't been free of him from the moment they'd met.

His eyes, dark and serious, wandered over her face. Before she could protest, he lowered his head and nuzzled her ear. "Why can't I get you out of my mind?"

"I can't answer that, either." He was going to kiss her again, in broad daylight, where they could be interrupted by anyone walking into the shop. Yet Savannah couldn't bring herself to break away, couldn't bring herself to put up so much as a token resistance.

A heartbeat later, his mouth drifted effortlessly over hers. It was as if he was afraid of what would happen and needed to slowly ease himself into the kiss. Softly he nibbled at her lips, each meeting of their mouths gaining in length and intensity until she parted to him, all but asking for his possession.

Dash groaned and, wrapping her more securely in his embrace, slid his tongue deep into her mouth to rove at will. She hung loosely in his arms, her hands dangling lifelessly at her sides.

"Dear, sweet heaven," he whispered as he broke off the kiss, groaning harshly. "It's even better than before."

Savannah said nothing, although she agreed. She was trembling, and prayed Dash didn't notice, but that was too much to ask. He slid his fingers into her hair and brought her face close to his, so they were cheek to cheek. "You're terrified, aren't you?"

"Don't be ridiculous," she snapped. She felt his smile against her flushed skin and realized she hadn't fooled him any more than she had herself. "I don't know what I am."

"I don't know, either. Somehow I wonder if I ever will. I don't suppose you'd make this process a whole lot easier and consider a wild, passionate love affair with me?"

Savannah stiffened, not knowing if he was serious. "Absolutely not."

"That's what I thought," he said and exhaled an elongated sigh. "It's going to be the whole nine yards with you, isn't it?"

"I'm sure I don't know what you mean."

"Perhaps not," he agreed reluctantly. Pulling away, he checked his watch and seemed surprised at the time.

"I've got to get back to the office. Later this afternoon I'll give Susan a call and the three of us can get together and make the necessary arrangements."

Savannah nodded. "We're going to have to move quickly. Planning for a wedding takes time."

"I know."

She smiled shyly, wanting him to realize how pleased she was with his change of heart. "This is very sweet of you, Dash."

He gestured weakly with his hands, as if he wasn't sure even now that he was doing the right thing. "I still think she's too young to be married. My sister's little more than a child. I can't help thinking she'll regret this someday."

"Marriage doesn't come with any guarantees at any age," Savannah felt obliged to tell him. "But then, neither does life. Susan and Kurt have an advantage you seem to be overlooking."

"What's that?"

"They're deeply in love."

"Love." Dash snickered loudly. "Generally it doesn't last more than two or three weeks."

"In some cases that's true, but not this time," Savannah said, reaching for a satin pillow the ring bearer would carry and holding it against her stomach. "I've worked with hundreds of couples over the years and I get a real sense about the people who come to me. Generally I can tell if their marriages will last or not."

"What about Kurt and Susan?"

"I believe they'll have a long, happy life together."

Dash rubbed the side of his face, his dark eyes intense. He didn't believe that. All he could do was build bridges with Susan and pray she was doing the right thing.

"Their love is strong."

Dash's responding smile was weak at best. "That was spoken like a true romantic."

"I'm hoping the skeptic in you will listen."

"I'm trying."

Savannah could see the truth in that. He was trying, for Susan's sake and perhaps her own. He'd come a long way from when they'd first met. But he had a lot farther to go.

Dash had no idea weddings could be so demanding, so expensive or so time-consuming. The one advantage to all this commotion and bother was the time he was able to spend with Savannah. What a prickly thing she was, defensive and wary. As the weeks progressed, Dash came to know Savannah Charles the businesswoman as well as he did the lovely, talented woman who'd first attracted him. He had to admit, she knew her stuff. He doubted that anyone else could have arranged so large and lavish a wedding on such short notice. It was only because she had a long-standing working relationship with those involved that Dash was able to give Susan an elaborate wedding.

As time passed, Dash lost count of how often he asked Savannah out to dinner, to a movie, a baseball game. She found a plausible excuse to decline each and every time. A less determined man would have grown discouraged and given up.

But no more, he mused, looking out his office window. As far as she was concerned, he held the trump card in the palm of his hot little hand. Savannah had conceded to attend Susan's wedding with him, and there was no way in hell he was letting her out of the agreement.

He sat at his desk, relaxed and calm, thinking about this final meeting that was scheduled for later that same afternoon. He'd been looking forward to it all week. Susan's wedding was taking place Saturday evening, and Savannah had flat run out of excuses.

Dash arrived at the shop before his sister. He was grateful for these few moments alone with Savannah.

"Hello, Dash." Savannah's face lit up with a ready smile when he walked into the shop. She was more relaxed with him now. She stood behind a silver punch bowl, decorating the perimeter with a strand of silk gardenias.

Her knack for making something ordinary strikingly beautiful was a rare gift. In some ways she'd done that with his life these past few weeks, giving him something to look forward to when he climbed out of bed. She'd challenged him, goaded him, irritated and bemused him. It took one hell of a woman to carry such a powerful punch.

"Susan's going to be a few minutes late," Dash told her, strolling into the shop. "I was hoping she'd had a change of heart and decided to call off the whole thing." He'd been doing nothing of the sort, but enjoyed getting a reaction out of Savannah.

"Give it up. Susan's going to make a beautiful bride."

"Who's going to be working the wedding?" he asked, advancing purposely toward her. He wouldn't agree to having her do so, not when she'd already consented to be his date.

"I am, of course."

He grinned, although he found no humor in her response. It was that he'd come to know her so well. He made an irritating buzzing sound. "Wrong."

"Dash, for the love of heaven will you kindly listen to reason? I can't be your date.... I know it's short notice but there are any number of women who'd enjoy—"

"We have an agreement," he reminded her.

"I realize that, but—"

"I won't take no for an answer, Savannah, not this time."

She stiffened, her back going ramrod straight. Dash had witnessed this particular reaction on numerous occasions. Whenever he asked her out, her prickly pride exploded into full bloom like a cactus flower. Damn but she had a streak of pure stubbornness as wide as the Mississippi River. Having continually butted heads with her, Dash was well acquainted with how well entrenched pride was in her.

"Dash, please."

He reached for her hand, gripping it with his own, and raised it to his lips. His mouth grazed her fingertips. "Not this time," he repeated. "I'll pick you up just before we meet to have the pictures taken."

"Dash..."

"Be ready, Savannah, because I swear I'll drag you there in your jeans and sweatshirt if I need to."

Savannah was in no mood for company, nor was she keen on talking to her mother when Joyce phoned that same evening. She'd done everything she could to talk Dash out of this madness. He insisted she be his date for Susan's wedding. Indeed, he'd blackmailed her into agreeing to it.

"I haven't heard from you in ages," her mother insisted.

"I've been busy with the last-minute details of Susan Davenport's wedding."

"She's Dash's sister, isn't she?"

Her mother knew the answer to that. She was looking for an excuse to drag Dash into the conversation, which she'd done countless times since meeting him. If she had to do that wager over again, she'd do it differently. Her entire day had been spent sloshing through regrets. She wanted to start over, be more patient, finish what she started, control her tongue, get out of this ridiculous "date" with Dash.

But she couldn't.

"Your father's talking about taking a trip to the ocean for a week or two."

"That sounds like an excellent idea." Savannah had been waiting all summer for them to get away.

"I'm not sure we should go."

"In the name of heaven, why not?" Savannah demanded impatiently.

"No reason. I hate to leave my garden, especially now when the tomatoes are starting to ripen. There have been a few break-ins in the neighborhood the last few weeks. I'd be too worried about the house to enjoy myself." The excuses were familiar enough for Savannah to want to scream with frustration. Her mother left out one very important reason for her uncertainty. She didn't want to leave Savannah. Naturally her parents had never come right out and said as much, but that was the underlying reason they stayed close to the Seattle area.

Countless times over the years Savannah had attempted to talk this out, but both her parents looked at her blankly as if she were being overly sensitive.

What they didn't realize was what poor liars they made.

"Have you seen much of Dash lately?" Her mother's voice rose expectantly.

"We've been working together on the wedding so we've actually been seeing a good deal of one another."

"I meant socially, dear. Has he taken you out on dates and the like? He's such a nice young man. Both your father and I think so."

"Mother," Savannah said, hating this, "I haven't been dating Dash."

Her mother's soft sigh of disappointment cut through Savannah like a chain saw. "I see."

"We're friends, nothing more."

"Of course. Be sure and let me know how the wedding goes, won't you?"

Seeing that Dash had spared little expense, it would be gorgeous. "I'll give you a call the first part of next week and tell you all about it."

"You promise?"

"Yes, Mom, I promise."

Savannah replaced the telephone receiver with a heavy heart. The load of guilt she carried was enough to buckle her knees. How could it be that one accident could have such a negative impact on so many people? It wasn't fair that her parents should continue to suffer years later for what had happened to her. Yet they blamed themselves, and that guilt was slowly destroying the best years of their lives.

Dash arrived to pick Savannah up late Saturday afternoon. He looked tall and distinguished in his black tuxedo and so damnably handsome that for an awkward moment, Savannah had trouble taking her eyes off him.

"What's wrong?" he said, running his finger along the inside of his starched collar. "I feel like a concert pianist."

Savannah couldn't keep from smiling. "I was just thinking how very distinguished you look."

His fingers went to his temple. "I'm going gray?"

"No." She laughed.

"*Distinguished* is the word a woman uses when the man's entering middle age and loses his hair."

"If you don't get us to this wedding, we're going to miss it, and then you really will lose your hair." She looped her arm in his and carefully placed one foot in front of the other. She rarely wore dress shoes. It was chancy at best, but she didn't want to ruin the effect of her full-length dress with ugly flats. Dash hadn't a clue at the time and effort she'd taken for this one date which was sure to be their first and last. She'd ordered the dress from New York, a soft, pale pink gown with a pearl-studded yoke. The long, sheer sleeves had layered pearl cuffs. She wore complementary pearl-stud earrings and a single-strand necklace.

It wasn't often in her life that Savannah felt beautiful, but she did now. She'd worked hard, wanting to make this evening special, knowing it would be her only date with Dash. She suspected there was a little bit of Cinderella in every woman, the need to believe in fairy tales and true love conquering against impossible odds. For this night, Savannah longed to forget she was crippled. For this night, she longed to pretend she was a beautiful princess.

Dash helped her across the yard and held open the door for her. She was inside the car, seat belt in place, when he joined her, his hands gripping the steering wheel. When he made no effort to start the car, she eyed him.

"Is something wrong?"

He turned and grinned at her, but she read the strain in his eyes and didn't understand it. "It's just that you're so damned beautiful, I can barely keep my hands off you."

"Oh, Dash," she whispered, fighting tears. "Thank you."

"For what?"

She shook her head, knowing she'd never be able to explain.

The church was gorgeous. Rarely had Savannah seen a sanctuary decorated more beautifully. The altar was surrounded with huge bouquets of pink and white roses and their scent filled the room like a warm incense. Dash had insisted on fresh flowers although the expense had been astronomical.

The end of each pew was decorated with a small bouquet of white rose buds and gardenias with silver and pink bows. The effect was breathtaking.

Seated in the front row, Savannah closed her eyes as the organ music swelled and filled the church. She stood and from the rustle of movement behind her, she knew the church was at capacity.

Savannah turned to see Dash escort his sister slowly down the center aisle, their steps in tune to the music that swelled through the sanctuary in triumphant waves of shared happiness.

Savannah had attended a thousand or more weddings in her years working as a coordinator. Yet it was always the same. The moment the music crescendoed, her eyes filled with tears at the beauty of it all.

This wedding was special because the bride was Dash's sister. Savannah had felt a part of it from the beginning, when Susan had come to her, desperate for assistance. Now it was all coming together and Susan was about to marry Kurt and become the wife of the man she truly loved.

Dash was uncomfortable with love, and a little jealous, too, although she doubted that he recognized it enough to deal with the negative emotion. Susan, the little sister he adored, was about to marry and move away to California with her husband.

When they reached the steps leading to the altar, Susan pressed a kiss on Dash's cheek before turning and placing her hand on Kurt's arm. Dash hesitated a moment as if he wasn't sure if he was ready to surrender his sister. Just when Savannah was beginning to get worried, he turned and entered the pew, standing next to her. Either by accident or design, his hand reached for hers. His grip was tight, his face strained with emotion.

Savannah was astonished to find his eyes bright with tears. She could easily be mistaken, since her own were blurred with happy emotion. A moment later, Savannah was convinced she was wrong.

The preacher made a few introductory comments about the sanctity of marriage. Holding his Bible open, he stepped forward. "I'd like each couple who's come to celebrate the union of Susan and Kurt to join hands," he instructed.

Dash reached for both of Savannah's hands so that she was forced to turn sideways. His eyes delved into hers and her heart seemed to stagger to a slow, uneven beat at what she read in them. Dash was an expert at disguising his feelings, at holding on to his anger and the pain of his long-dead marriage, at keeping that bitterness alive. As he stared down at her, his eyes became bright and clear and filled with emotion so strong, it transcended anything she'd ever known.

Savannah was barely aware of what was going on around them. Sounds faded into thin threads; even the soloist who was singing seemed to be floating away. Savannah's peripheral vision became clouded, as if she'd stepped into a dreamworld. Her sole focus was Dash.

With her hands joined to Dash's, their eyes linked, the pastor instructed, "For those of you wishing to renew your vows, repeat after me."

Dash's fingers squeezed hers. "I promise before God and all those gathered here this day to take you as my wife. I promise to love and cherish you, to leave my heart and my life open to you."

To Savannah's amazement, Dash stated the words in a low, husky whisper. She could hear others around them doing the same. Once again tears filled her eyes. How easy it would be to pretend he was devoting himself to her.

"I'll treasure you as a gift from God, to encourage you to be all He meant for you to be," Savannah found herself stating a few moments later. "I promise to share your dreams, to appreciate your talents, to respect you. I pledge myself to you, to learn from and value our differences." As her voice faded, Savannah's heart beat strong and steady and sure. An excitement filled her as she realized what she'd said was true. These were the very things she yearned to do for Dash. She longed for him to trust her enough to allow her into his life, to help him bury the hurts of the past. They were different, as different as any couple could be. That didn't make their relationship impossible. It added flavor, texture and challenge to their attraction. Life together would never be dull for them.

"I promise to give you the very best of myself, to be faithful to you, to be your friend and your partner," Dash whispered next, his voice gaining strength. A ring of sincerity echoed through his words.

"I offer you my heart and my love," Savannah repeated, her own heart ready to burst open with unrestrained joy.

"You are my friend," Dash returned, "my lover, my wife."

It was as if they, too, were part of the ceremony, as if they, too, were pledging their love and their lives for all time to each other.

Through the words of a preacher, Savannah offered Dash all that she had to give. It wasn't until they'd finished and the pastor instructed Kurt to kiss his bride that Savannah realized this wasn't real. She'd stepped into a dreamworld, the fantasy one she'd created out of her own futile need for love. Dash had only been following the lead of the minister. Mortified, she lowered her gaze and tugged her trembling fingers free from Dash's.

He, too, apparently harbored regrets. His hands reached for and tightened around the pew in front of them until his knuckles paled. He formed a fist with his right hand. Savannah dared not look up at him, certain he'd read her thoughts and fearing she'd know his. She couldn't have borne the disappointment. For the next several hours they'd be forced to share each other's company, through the dinner and the dance that followed the ceremony. Savannah didn't know how she was going to manage it now, after she'd humiliated herself.

Thankfully she was spared having to face Dash immediately following the ceremony. He became a part of the reception line that welcomed friends and relatives. Savannah was busy herself, working with the woman she'd hired to coordinate the wedding and reception. Together they took down the pew bows, which would serve as floral centerpieces for the dinner which was to follow.

"I don't know when I've attended a more beautiful wedding ceremony," Nancy Mastell told Savannah, working furiously. "You'd think I'd be immune to this after all the ceremonies we attend."

"It . . . was beautiful," Savannah agreed. Her stomach was in knots, and her battered heart recognized how foolish she'd been; nevertheless, she couldn't make herself regret what had happened. She'd learned something about herself, something she'd denied far too long. She needed love in her life, the same way oxygen was necessary for her to breathe. For years she'd cut herself off from opportunity, content to live off the happiness of others. For years she'd been like a robot, moving from one day into the next, lugging her pains and disappointments with her, never truly happy, never fulfilled. Pretending.

This was why Dash threatened her. She couldn't pretend with him. Instinctively he knew. For reasons she would probably never understand, he saw straight through her.

"Let me get those," Nancy said. "You're a wedding guest."

"I can help." But Nancy insisted otherwise.

When Savannah returned to the vestibule, she found Dash waiting for her. They drove in silence to the plush restaurant Dash had rented for the evening, where dinner was to be served.

Savannah prayed Dash would say something to cut the terrible tension. She could think of nothing herself. A long list of possible topics of conversation presented itself, but she couldn't find a single one that didn't sound silly and overused.

Heaven help her, she didn't know how it would be possible for them to spend the rest of the evening in each other's company.

The dinner proved to be less of problem than Savannah expected. They were seated at a table with two delightful older gentlemen that Dash introduced to her as John Stackhouse and Arnold Sterle, the senior partners of the law firm that employed Dash.

"Mighty fine wedding," the older of the two told Dash.

"Thank you. I wish I could take the credit, but it's the fruit of Savannah's efforts you're seeing."

"Beautiful wedding," Stackhouse went on to say. "I can't remember when I've enjoyed another one more."

Savannah was waiting for a sarcastic remark from Dash, but one never came. She didn't dare hope that he'd changed his opinion, and guessed it had something to do with the elderly men who were seated with them.

Savannah spread the linen napkin across her lap. When she looked up, she discovered Arnold Sterle studying her. She wondered if her mascara had run or if there was something wrong with her makeup. Her doubts must have read in her eyes, because he grinned and winked at her.

Savannah blushed. A sixty-five-year-old corporate attorney was actually flirting with her. It took her an amazingly short time to recover enough to wink back at him.

Arnold burst out in loud chuckles, attracting the attention of Dash and John Stackhouse. The other elderly gentleman glanced disapprovingly at his law partner. "Something troubling you, Arnold?"

"Just that I wish I were thirty years younger. Savannah here's prettier than a picture."

"You been nipping at the bottle again, haven't you?" his friend asked. "He becomes something of a flirt when he does," the other man explained.

Arnold's cheeks puffed with outrage. "I most certainly have not."

Their tossed green salads were delivered and Savannah noted, from the corner of her eye, that Dash was closely studying her. Taking her chances, she turned and met his gaze. To her surprise, he smiled and reached for her hand under the table.

"Old Arnold's right," he whispered close to her ear. "Every other woman here fades compared to you."

The orchestra was tuning their instruments in the distance and Savannah focused her attention on the group of musicians as regret and frustration filled her. "There's something you should know," she said, holding the napkin close to her mouth.

"What now?"

"I'm sorry, I can't dance. But please don't let that stop you."

"I'm not much of a dancer myself. Don't worry about it."

"Anything wrong?" Arnold asked.

"No, no," Dash was quick to answer. "Savannah had a quick question."

"I see."

"There's something we've been meaning to discuss with you, Dash. Now seems as good a time as any. It's about the position for senior partner opening up at the firm," John said.

"Can't we leave business out of this evening?" Arnold asked, before Dash could respond. Arnold frowned with dissatisfaction. "It's a difficult enough task choosing another partner without worrying about it day and night."

Dash didn't need to say a word for Savannah to know how much he wanted the position. She felt it in him, the way his body tensed, the eager way his head inclined at the mention of the subject.

The dinner dishes were cleared from the table by the expert staff. The music started, a wistful number that reminded Savannah of sweet wine and red roses. Susan, in her flowing silk gown, danced with Kurt as their guests looked on approvingly.

The following number Kurt danced with his mother and Dash with Susan. His assurances that he wasn't much of a dancer proved to be false. He was wonderfully graceful.

Savannah must have looked more wistful than she realized because when the next number was announced, Arnold Sterle reached for her hand. "The next dance is mine."

Savannah was too flabbergasted to speak. "I... can't. I'm sorry, but I can't."

"Nonsense." With that, the smiling older man reached for her hand and all but pulled her from her chair.

Chapter Six

Savannah was close to tears. She couldn't dance and now she was being forced onto the a huge ballroom-style floor by a sweet old man who didn't understand she was lame. Humiliation burned her cheeks. The wonderful romantic fantasy she was living was about to blow up in her face. Then, when she least expected to be rescued, Dash was at her side, his hand at her elbow.

"I believe this dance is mine, Mr. Sterle," he said, whisking Savannah away from the table.

Relief surged through her, until she realized he was escorting her onto the dance floor himself. "Dash, I can't," she insisted in a heated whisper. "Please don't ruin this day for me."

"Do you trust me?"

"Yes, but you don't seem to understand...."

Understand or not, he led her confidently onto the crowded floor, turned and gathered her in his arms. "All I want you to do is relax. I'll do all the real work."

"Dash!"

"Relax, will you?"

"No... Please take me back to the table." He didn't seem to grasp what he was asking of her.

He captured her hands and raised them, tucking them around his neck and holding them prisoner there. Savannah hung her head and turned her face away from him. Their bodies fit snugly against each other and Dash felt warm and substantive. His thigh moved against hers, his chest brushed her breasts and a slow, uneasy excitement began to build within her. After holding her breath, she released it in a long, trembling sigh.

"It feels good, doesn't it?"

"Yes." She couldn't very well lie.

"We're going to make this as simple and easy as possible. All you need to do is hold on to me." He held her close, his hands knotted at the base of her spine. "This isn't so bad now, is it?"

"I'll never forgive you for this, Dashiel Davenport." Savannah was afraid to breathe again for fear she'd stumble, for fear she'd embarrass them both. She'd never been on a dance floor in her life and try as she might, she couldn't make herself relax the way he wanted. This was foreign territory to her. The girl who'd never been asked to a school dance. The girl who'd watched and envied her friends from afar. The girl who'd only waltzed in her dreams with imaginary partners. And not one of them had been anything like Dash.

"Maybe this will help," Dash whispered. He bent his head and kissed the side of her neck with his warm, moist mouth.

"Dash!" She squirmed against him.

"I've been longing to do that all night," he whispered. Goose bumps shivered up her arms as his tongue made lazy circles over the contour of her ear. Her knees felt like jelly and she involuntarily pressed her weight against him.

"Please stop that!" she said between clenched teeth.

"Not on your life. You're doing great." He made the majority of the moves and, holding her the way he was, took the weight off her injured leg so that she could slide with him.

"I'll embarrass us both any minute," she insisted, but not quite as strenuously.

"Close your eyes and enjoy the music."

Since they were in the middle of the floor, Savannah had no choice but to follow his instructions. Her chance to gracefully escape had long since passed.

The music was wonderful, slow and easy, and when she lowered her lashes, she could pretend. This was the night, she'd decided earlier, to play the role of the princess. Only she'd never expected her Cinderella fantasy to make it all the way to the ballroom floor.

"You're a natural," Dash whispered. "Why have you waited so long?"

She was barely moving, which was all she could manage. This was her first experience, and although she was loath to admit it, Dash was right, she was doing very well. This must be a dream, a wonderful romantic dream. If so, she prayed it'd be a very long time before she woke.

As she relaxed, Dash's arms eased to a more comfortable position. She pressed her arm across his shoulder and her fingers toyed with the short hairs at the base of his neck. It was a small but intimate gesture, to run her fingers through his hair, and she wondered at her courage. It might be just another facet of her fantasy, but it seemed the action of a lover or a wife.

Wife.

The word went through her like a steel blade. In the church, when they'd repeated the vows, Dash had called her his friend, his lover, his wife. It wasn't real. She didn't need shock therapy to remind her of how unreal it had all been. But for now, this moment, she was in his arms and they were dancing cheek to cheek, as naturally as if they'd been partners for years. For now, she would make it real, because she so badly wanted to believe it.

"Who said you couldn't dance?" Dash asked her after a while.

"Shh." She didn't want to talk. These moments were much too precious to waste on conversation. This time was meant to be savored and enjoyed. It would have to hold her through the long, empty years that stretched before her like a black hole.

The song ended and when the next one started almost without pause, the beat was fast paced and loud. Her small bubble of happiness burst. The regret must have shone in her eyes because Dash chuckled and placed his hand under her chin. "If we can waltz, we can do this."

"Dash . . . I was able to do the slow dances because you were holding me, but this is impossible."

Dash, however, wasn't listening. He was dancing. Without her. His arms jerked back and forth in opposite directions, his elbows working in and out in a seesawing action. His feet seemed to be following the same haphazard course. He laughed and threw back his head. "Go for it, Savannah!" He shouted to be heard above the music. "Don't just stand there like a bump on a log. Dance."

She was going to need to move, and quickly. Off the dance floor. She was about to turn away when Dash gripped her by the waist, holding her with both hands. "You can't quit now."

"Oh, yes, I can. Just watch me."

"All you need to do is move a little to the rhythm. You don't need to leap across the dance floor."

There was no talking to the man, so she tossed her arms in the air in abject frustration.

"That's it," he shouted enthusiastically.

"Excuse me, excuse me," Arnold Sterle's voice said from behind her. "Dash, would you mind very much if I danced with Savannah now?" he shouted.

Dash looked at Savannah and grinned, as bright and cheerful as a six-year-old pulling a prank on his first-grade teacher. "Savannah would love to dance with you. Isn't that right?" With that, he bebopped his way off the floor, his legs and arms kicking as he went.

"I'm not much for this loud music," Arnold Sterle said, reaching behind his ear and adjusting his hearing aid. "It takes the wax right out of my ears."

Savannah didn't mean to laugh, but she couldn't stop herself. "I'm not much good at this myself."

"Shall we, then?" he said, holding out his palm to her.

Reluctantly she placed her hand in his. She didn't want to offend Dash's boss, especially when he was such an adorable fellow. But she didn't want to embarrass herself, either. Taking Dash's advice, she moved her arms, just a little at first, convinced she looked like a chicken attempting flight. Others around her were wiggling and twisting every which direction. Savannah's movements, or lack of them, weren't likely to be noticed.

To her utter amazement, Mr. Sterle set one foot in front of the other in a scissor-type action and started to twist back and forth. With each jerking motion he sank a little closer to the floor, until he was practically kneeling. After a moment he didn't move. He resembled a statue, frozen, one arm stretched forward, one elbow back.

"Mr. Sterle, are you all right?"

"Would you mind helping me up? My back seems to have gone out on me."

Savannah looked frantically about the room for Dash, but he was nowhere to be seen. She was silently calling him several colorful names for getting her into this predicament. With no help for it, she bent forward, tucked her hand around the older man's elbow and helped him into an upright position.

"Thanks," he said, and beamed her a bright smile. "I got carried away there and forgot I'm an old man. Damn, but it felt good. My heart hasn't beat this fast in years."

"Maybe we should sit down," she suggested, praying he'd agree.

"Not on your life, young lady. I'm only getting started."

* * *

Dash made his way back to the table, smiling to himself. He hadn't meant to embarrass Savannah. His original intent had been to rescue her. Taking her onto the dance floor had been pure impulse. He'd been looking for an excuse to hold her all night, and he wasn't about to throw away what could prove to be his only chance.

Beautiful didn't begin to describe Savannah. When he'd first met her, he'd thought of her as cute, pixie-like. He'd dated women far more attractive than she was. On looks alone, she wasn't the type that stood out in a crowd. Nor did she have the voluptuous body of a temptress. She was small, short and proportioned accordingly. If he was looking for long shapely legs and an ample bust line, he wouldn't find either in Savannah. She wasn't a beauty, and yet she was the most beautiful woman he'd ever known.

That didn't make a lot of sense, he realized. He owed it to the fact that he'd never met anyone quite like Savannah Charles. He didn't fully understand why she appealed so strongly to him. True, she had the heart of a lioness, a determination of steel and courage unlike any he'd ever known.

"Is Arnold out there making a world-class fool of himself?" John Stackhouse asked, when Dash joined the elder of the two senior partners at the dinner table.

"He's dancing with Savannah."

John Stackhouse was by far the most dignified and reserved of the two senior partners. Both were widowers and members of the executive committee, which had the final say on the appointment of the next senior partner. Stackhouse was often the most disapproving of the pair. He liked things done in the proper manner. Over the years, Dash had butted heads with him on more than one occasion. Their views on certain issues invariably clashed. Although he wasn't particularly fond of the older man, Dash respected him, and considered him fair-minded.

John Stackhouse sipped from his wineglass. "Actually, I'm pleased we can have this time to talk," he said to Dash, arching a thick eyebrow. "A wedding's not the place to bring up business, I realize that, but I believe now might be a very good time for the two of us to talk about the senior partnership."

The oxygen froze in Dash's lungs, and he nodded. "I'd appreciate that."

"You've been with the firm several years now, and worked hard. We've won some valuable cases because of you, and that's all in your favor."

"I'm glad to hear that." So Paul Justice didn't have it all sewn up the way he'd assumed.

"I don't generally offer advice."

This was true enough. Stackhouse kept his opinions to himself until asked, and it bode well that he was willing to make a few suggestions to Dash. Although he badly wanted the position, Dash didn't think he had a ghost of a chance against Paul Justice. "I'd appreciate any advice you care to give me."

Although he sipped from his wine as if to suggest the alcohol had prompted this tête-à-tête, Dash knew otherwise. Old Stackhouse was as alert and astute as ever.

"Arnold and a couple of the other members of the executive committee were discussing names. Yours was raised almost immediately."

Dash scooted so close to the end of his chair, he was in danger of falling off. "What's the consensus?"

"Off-the-record."

"Off-the-record," Dash assured him.

"You're liked and respected, but there's a problem, a big one as far as the firm's concerned. The fact is, I was the one who brought it up, and the others claimed to have noticed it, as well."

"Yes?" Dash's mind zoomed over the list of potential areas of trouble.

"You've been divorced several years now."

"Yes."

"This evening's the first time I've seen you put that failure behind you. I've watched you chew on your bitterness like an old bone, digging it up and showing it off like a prized possession when it suited you. You've developed a cutting and sarcastic edge. That's fine in the courtroom, but a detriment in your professional life as well as your private life. Especially if you're serious about this senior partnership."

"I am serious," Dash was quick to assure him, too quick perhaps because Stackhouse smiled. That happened so rarely it was worth noting.

"I'm glad to hear you say that."

"Is there anything I could do to help my chances?" This conversation was unprecedented, something Dash had never believed possible.

The well-known and respected attorney hesitated and glanced toward the dance floor and frowned. "How serious are you about this young woman?"

Of all the things Dash had expected to hear, this surprised him the most. "Ah..." Dash wasn't a man who floundered with words, but he hadn't a clue how to answer. "I don't know. Why do you ask?"

"I realize it's presumptuous of me, and I do hope you'll forgive me, but it might sway matters considerably if you were to marry again."

"Marry?" he repeated, as if the word were foreign to him.

"It would show the committee that you've put the past behind you," John continued, "and that you're looking to build a more positive future."

"I see."

"Naturally, there are no guarantees and I certainly wouldn't suggest you consider marriage if you weren't already thinking along those lines. I wouldn't have said anything, but I noticed the way you were dancing with the young lady and it seemed to me you care deeply for her."

"She's special."

The other man smiled gently. "Indeed she is. Would you mind terribly if I danced with her myself? I see no reason for Arnold to have all the fun." Not waiting for Dash to respond, he stood and made his way across the dance floor to Savannah and his friend.

Dash watched as John Stackhouse tapped his fellow attorney on the shoulder and cut in. Savannah smiled softly as the second man claimed her.

Marry!

Dash rubbed a hand down his face. A few months earlier, the suggestion would have infuriated him. A few months earlier, he hadn't met Savannah.

Nor had he stood in a church, held hands with an incredible woman and repeated vows. Vows meant for his sister and the man she loved. Not him. Not Savannah. Yet these vows had come straight from his heart to hers. He had intended it to be that way. Not in the beginning. All he wanted to do was show Savannah how far he'd come. Echoing a few words seemed such a small thing at the time.

But it wasn't as simple as all that. The words had opened the doors of his emptiness. Nothing had seemed real from that moment forward. He'd spoken in a haze, not fully comprehending the effect it had on him. All he understood was that he was tired. Tired of being alone. Tired of pretending he didn't need anyone else. Tired of playing a game in which he was the guaranteed loser. Those vows he'd stated with Savannah had described the kind of marriage Savannah believed in so strongly. The ideal.

He knew that, but for the first time in years he was willing to admit it was feasible for a man and a woman to share this rare, mutually respected partnership. Savannah had made that real to him the moment she'd repeated the vows herself.

Marry Savannah.

He waited for the revulsion to hit him the way it generally did when someone mentioned the word *marriage*. Nothing happened. Of course, this was perfectly logical. He'd spent valuable time in a wedding shop, making a multitude of decisions that revolved around Susan's wedding. He'd become immune to the negative jolt the word generally struck in him.

But he expected some adverse reaction. A twinge, a shiver of doubt. Something.

It didn't come.

Marriage, he repeated again slowly in his mind, letting his conscience mull over the true meaning of the word. He'd never consider anything so drastic. Not for the sole reason of making senior partner. He'd worked hard, damn hard. It was a natural progression. If he didn't get the appointment now, he would sometime later.

Marriage to Savannah. By heaven, if there was ever a time when the wine was talking, it was now.

Savannah couldn't remember a night she'd enjoyed more. She'd danced and drank champagne, then danced again. Every time she'd turned around there was someone there looking to dance with her or fill her glass.

"Oh, Dash, I had the most incredible night of my life," she said, leaning her head against the headrest in his car and closing her eyes. It was a mistake, because the world went on a crazy spin.

"It was that good, was it?"

"Yes, oh, yes. I hate for it to end."

"Then why should it? Where would you like to go?"

"You'll take me anywhere?"

"Name it."

"The beach. I want to go to the beach." She was making a fool of herself, but she didn't care. She wanted to throw out her arms and sing. Where was a mountaintop when she needed one?

"Your wish is my command," Dash said to her.

She slipped her hand around his upper arm and hugged him, leaning her head against his shoulder. "This's the way I feel about this night. It's magical. I could ask for anything and somehow it would be given to me."

"I believe it would."

Excited now that her fantasy had become so very real, she rolled down the car window and let out a wild whoop of unrestrained joy.

Dash laughed. "What was that for?"

"I'm so happy. My goodness, I never dreamed I could dance like that. Did you see me? Did you see all the men who asked me?" She pressed her hand over her breast. "Me. I always thought I could never dance, and I did, and I owe it all to you."

"I knew you could."

"But how... I'd never dared to hope."

"You can walk, can't you?"

"Yes, but I assumed it was impossible to actually dance." The champagne had gone to her head, but she welcomed the light-headedness it produced. "Oh, my, did you see Mr. Stackhouse? I thought I'd burst out laughing. I'm convinced he's never done the jitterbug in his life. He looked at me and I looked at him and before I could suggest we sit out the next dance, he started doing a wild version of jumping jacks." The memory produced a giggle. "I don't know who was more surprised, him or me."

"I couldn't believe my eyes," Dash said and she heard the amusement in his voice. "Neither could Arnold Sterle. Arnold claimed they've been friends for thirty-five years and he's never seen John do anything like it, claimed he was just trying to outdo him. I believe that was when Mr. Sterle leapt onto the dance floor and the three of you started the conga line."

"There is magic to this night, isn't there?"

"There must be," he agreed.

Her leg should be aching, and would be soon, but she hadn't experienced so much as a twinge. Perhaps later when adrenaline wasn't pumping through her body and she was back on the planet Earth, she'd experience the familiar discomfort. But it hadn't happened yet.

"Your beach," Dash announced, edging into the parking space at Alki Beach in West Seattle. A wide expanse of sandy beach stretched before them. Seattle city lights flickered in the distance like decorations on a gaily lit Christmas tree. Gentle waves lapped the driftwood-strewn shore. The scents of salt and seaweed hung in the air. "Make all your wishes this easy to fulfill, will you?"

"I'll do my best," she promised. Her list was short, shockingly short for a woman who, for this one night, was a princess in disguise.

"Any other easy requests?" Dash asked. He scooted close and draped his arm across her shoulders.

"A full moon would be nice."

"Will a crescent-shaped one do, as well?"

"It'll have to."

"Perhaps I could find a way to make it up to you," Dash suggested, his voice low and oddly breathless.

"It's all right," she said, feeling generous. "This moon will do just as well."

"I was thinking of ways to take your mind off the moon."

"Oh?" Oh, please let him kiss me, Savannah pleaded to the powers that be. The night would be perfect if only Dash were to take her in his arms and kiss her as if it'd take a lifetime to meet his need for her.

"Do you know what I'm thinking?" he asked, his words a silken thread near her ear.

She closed her eyes and nodded. "Kiss me, Dash. Please kiss me."

His mouth came down on hers and she thought she was ready for the sensual invasion, since she'd yearned for it so badly. Nothing could have prepared her for the greed they experienced for each other. She opened to him, linked her arms around his neck and gave herself to his touch. He thrust his tongue deep inside her mouth, tasting, stroking, battling, until she whimpered in surrender. He tasted so damn good—a mixture of champagne and wedding cake. Sweet and potent. Power and passion. The mixture was a heady one that left her clawing her fingers through his hair.

"Why is it," Dash groaned, as he breathed kisses across her cheeks and lower lip, "that we seem to be forevermore kissing in a car?"

"I . . . don't know."

His lips toyed with hers, taking her lower one between his own and then unmercifully teasing her upper one with the tip of his tongue. "You're making this damned difficult."

"I am." She kneaded the muscles beneath his shirt, amazed at the strength she felt in him. Being with him like this made her strong, and for a woman who'd felt weak most of her life, this was a potent aphrodisiac.

"You're so damned beautiful," Dash whispered, just before his mouth devoured hers in a kiss that left her panting and breathless. A kiss that left her yearning for much more.

"For tonight I'm invincible," she agreed. Privately she wondered if Cinderella had ever had a time like this with her prince before rushing away and leaving him with a single glass slipper. She wondered if her counterpart had the opportunity to experience such unexpected pleasure. Or had Cinderella lived like Savannah, locked in a dungeon of doubts?

Dash kissed her again and again, until a host of dizzying sensations accosted her from all sides and she broke away and buried her face in his chest in a desperate effort to clear her head.

"Savannah." Taking her by the shoulders, he eased himself away from her. "Look at me."

Blindly she obeyed him, running her tongue over her mouth that was swollen from the urgency of their kisses. "Touch me," she pleaded at the desire she read in his eyes, the desire that was a reflection of her own. "The way you did before."

Dash went still, his breathing labored. "I can't.... We're on a public beach." His hands eased upward to the underside of her breasts and his touch was as electric as his kisses had been.

He closed his eyes, drew in a deep breath and bared his teeth. "That does it," he said forcefully, pulling away from her. "We're going to do this right. We're not teenagers anymore. I want to make love to you, Savannah, and I'm not willing to risk being interrupted by a policeman who'll arrest me for indecent liberties." He reached for the ignition and started the car, but not before she noticed how badly his hand shook.

"Where are we going?"

"My house."

"Dash..."

"Don't argue with me."

"Kiss me first," she instructed, not understanding his angry impatience. They had all night. She wouldn't turn back into a pumpkin for several hours yet.

"I have every intention of kissing you. The fact is, I'm going to kiss you in places you've never been kissed before."

"That sounds nice," she whispered, and with a soft sigh pressed her head against his shoulder.

"You'll like it, I promise."

"I'm not always beautiful." She thought it was only fair to tell him that. "Or desirable."

"I hate to argue with you, especially now," he said, planting one last kiss on the corner of her mouth, "but I disagree."

"I'm really not," she insisted, although she thought it was very gentlemanly of him to disagree.

"I want you more than I've ever wanted another woman in my life."

"You do?" It was so beautiful of him to say such things, but it wasn't necessary. Unexpected tears filled her eyes. "No one's ever said things like that to me before."

"Stupid fools." They stopped at a red light and Dash reached for her and kissed her as if he longed to make up for a lifetime of cruel rejections. No man had ever been so passionate, or so desperate for her. Savannah linked her arms around his neck and sighed when he finally broke off the kiss.

"You're not drunk, are you?" Dash demanded, turning a corner sharply. He shot a wary glance at her, as if this was a recent suspicion.

"No." She was just a little, but not enough to taint her judgment. "I know exactly what I'm doing."

"Right, but do you know what I intend on doing?"

"Yes, you're taking me home so we can make wild, passionate love in your bed. You'd prefer that to being arrested for doing so publicly."

"Smart girl."

"I'm not a girl!"

"Sorry, it was a slip of the tongue. Trust me, I know exactly how much of a woman you are."

"No, you don't. You haven't a clue, Dash Davenport, but that's all right because no one else does, either." Herself included, but she didn't say that.

Dash pulled into his driveway and was apparently going faster than he realized, because when he hit his brakes the car came to an abrupt stop. "The way I've been driving, it's a miracle I didn't get a ticket," he mumbled apparently to himself as he leapt out of the car. He opened her door, and Savannah lazily smiled and lifted her arms to him.

"I don't know if I can walk," she said with a tired sigh. "I can dance, though, if anyone cares to ask."

He scooted her effortlessly into his arms, and with quick steps, carried her onto his front porch. Savannah was curious to see his home, curious to learn everything she could about him. She wanted to remember every second of this incredible night.

It was a bit awkward getting the key into the lock and holding her at the same time, but Dash managed. He threw open the door and walked into the dark room. He hesitated, kicked the door closed and traipsed across the living room, not bothering to turn on the lights.

"Stop," she insisted.

"For what? Savannah, for the love of heaven, you're driving me crazy."

"Sexually, or because I'm making unreasonable demands on you?"

"Sexually."

Languishing in his arms, she arched back her head and kissed his cheek. "What a romantic thing to say."

"You wanted something?" he asked impatiently.

"Oh, yes, I want to see your home. A person learns a great deal about someone just by noticing the kind of furniture a person buys. Little things, too, like the design of their dishes. I've been curious about you from the start."

"You want to know the pattern of my china?"

"You'd rather make love, wouldn't you?" she asked, mildly disappointed.

"That's an understatement if ever I heard one."

Dash moved expertly down the darkened hallway to his room. Gently he placed her on the mattress and knelt over her. She smiled up at him. "Oh, Dash, you have a poster bed. I've always wanted to make love in a big, four-poster bed."

"As I said earlier, your wish is my command." He sat on the edge of the mattress and peeled off his jacket. His tie followed. Next he jerked the shirt free of his waist, but was all thumbs with the fancy buttons.

"Let me help you."

"I can get it," he said, sounding both anxious and impatient.

Struggling into a sitting position, Savannah stretched her arms behind her in a effort to release the small loop button at the base of her neck. "This shouldn't take long," she promised.

Dash was having problems of his own, and revealed none of the care he'd shown seconds earlier. When he couldn't manage to unfasten the buttons, he eased his arms from the sleeves until they bounced like crazed puppets at his sides. Savannah couldn't help laughing at his frantic efforts.

"You think this is funny, do you?"

"I'm sorry, really I am." She wasn't, but she didn't want him to know that.

"Houdini couldn't have gotten out of this stupid shirt. I swear these work better than straitjackets."

"Here." She knelt next to him and eased the fabric free. "Don't be so impatient. We have all night."

"And tomorrow."

"No," she corrected. "This will only work for this one night. The magic ends at midnight and then the princess disappears and I go back to being a pumpkin." Dash froze and his gaze collided with hers, before he groaned and fell backward onto the mattress. "You are drunk, aren't you?"

"No," she insisted. "Just happy. Now kiss me and quit asking so many questions." She was reaching for him when it happened. The pain shot like fire through her leg and, groaning, she fell onto her side.

Chapter Seven

Dash recognized the supreme effort Savannah made to hide her pain. It must have been excruciating, certainly much too intense to disguise. Lying on her back, she squeezed her eyes tightly closed, gritted her teeth and then attempted to manage the agony with deep-breathing exercises.

"Savannah," he whispered, not wanting to break her concentration and at the same time desperately needing to do something, anything to ease her discomfort. "Let me help," he pleaded.

She shook her head from side to side. "It'll pass in a few minutes."

Even in the moonlight, Dash could see how pale she'd become. He jumped off the bed and was pacing like a wild beast, feeling the searing grip of her pain himself. It twisted at his stomach muscles, producing a mental torment unlike anything he'd ever experienced.

"Let me massage your leg," he insisted, and when she didn't protest he lifted the skirt of her full-length gown and ran his hands up and down her thigh. Her skin was hot to the touch and when he placed his chilled hands on her heated flesh, she groaned anew.

"It'll pass," he whispered reassuringly, praying he was right. His heart was pounding at double time in his anxiety. He couldn't bear to see Savannah endure this unbearable pain, and stand by and do nothing.

Her thigh was terribly scarred and his heart ached at the agony she'd endured over the years. Her muscles were tense and knotted but gradually began to relax as he gently worked her flesh with both hands, easing them up and down her thigh and calf. He saw the marks of several surgeries; their scars were testament to her suffering and her bravery.

"There are pills in my purse," she whispered, her voice barely discernible.

Her purse! Dash quickly surveyed the room, jerking his head from left to right, wondering where she'd set it. He found it on the carpet next to the bed. Grasping it, he emptied the contents on top of the mattress. The brown plastic bottle filled with a prescription for muscle relaxers rolled into view.

Hurrying into his bathroom, he poured her a glass of water and dumped a handful of the thick chalky tablets into the palm of his hand. "Here," he said.

Levering herself up on one elbow, Savannah reached for three of the pills. Her hands were trembling, he noted, and it was all he could do to resist taking her in his arms. Once she downed the pills, she closed her eyes and rested her head against the pillow.

"Take me home, please."

"In a few minutes. Let's give those pills a chance to work first."

She was sobbing softly, openly now. Dash lay down next to her and gathered her in his arms. She fit snugly in his embrace, her head tucked against his shoulder.

"I'm sorry," she sobbed.

"For what?"

"For ruining everything. Midnight came much too soon."

He brushed his lips over the crown of her head. "Midnight?" It was well past that now and had been for hours.

"I turned back into a pumpkin. I...didn't want you to see my thigh." Her tears were in earnest now and she buried her face in his shoulder.

"Why? It's part of you, a very important part."

"It's ugly."

"You're beautiful."

"For one night...but only until midnight."

"You're wrong, Savannah. You're beautiful every minute of every day." He cradled her head against him, whispering softly in her ear. Gradually he felt the terrible tension ease from her and he knew by the even sound of her breathing that she was drifting off to sleep.

Dash held her for several moments, wondering what he should do. She'd asked that he take her home, but waking her seemed cruel, especially now that the terrible agony had passed. She needed her sleep, and movement might bring back the pain.

What it boiled down to, he realized reluctantly, was a simple fact he'd rather not admit. He wanted Savannah with him and was unwilling to relinquish her.

Kissing her temple, he eased himself from her arms and crawled off the bed. He brought down a thick blanket from the top shelf in his closet and covered her with it, careful to tuck the fullness about her shoulders.

She resembled a slumbering child, curled up in a tight ball. Looking down on her, Dash buried his hands in his pockets and stared for several moments while emotions circled him like the thick rope of a lasso.

He'd been minutes away from positioning himself over her and making love to her, minutes away from burying himself in the warmth of her sex and enjoying the pleasure their bodies could bring each other. Dash had been eager and thoughtless, forgetting her special needs. It angered him now that he could have been so careless. Savannah wasn't like other women, and the differences didn't stop with the physical.

Breaking into a cold sweat at how narrowly he'd diverted disaster, he reached for a shirt. Buttoning it, he wandered into the living room, slumped into his recliner and sat in the dark while the night shadows moved against the opposite wall.

He'd been careless and inconsiderate, but mostly he'd been irresponsible. Bringing Savannah to his home had been the last in a long list of errors in his judgment.

He was drunk, but not on champagne. His intoxication was strictly due to a prolonged exposure to a warm, gentle Savannah. The idealist. The romantic. Attending his sister's wedding hadn't helped matters any. Susan had been a beautiful bride and if there was ever a time he could believe in the power of love and the strength of vows, it was this day.

It'd started early in the evening when he'd exchanged vows with Savannah as if *they* were the ones who were to be married. It was a moment out of time—unreal and dangerous.

He'd attempted to reckon what had happened, offered an endless litany of excuses, but he wasn't sure he'd ever find one that would satisfy him. He wished there were someone or something he could put his finger on and blame, but that wasn't likely to happen. The best he could hope for was to forget the whole episode and pray Savannah did the same.

Savannah. She was so damned beautiful. He'd never enjoyed dancing with a woman the way he did her. Smiling to himself, he recalled that he wasn't the only one caught up in the magic of her joy. Being with her, sharing this night with her, was like being sucked into the magic of a fairy tale, impossible to resist even if he'd cared to try. And he hadn't.

Before he knew what was happening, they were parked at Alki Beach, kissing like there was no tomorrow, with visions of her naked beneath him filling his head. He'd never desired a woman more.

Wrong. His mind made an irritating buzzing sound. There had been a time, years earlier, when he'd been equally enthralled with a woman. In retrospect it was easy to pardon his naïveté. He was young and impressionable. His single and biggest mistake had been the fact that he'd been hopelessly in love.

Love. He didn't even like the sound of the word. It stuck in his mind the way a fish bone does in a throat. He'd found love to be very much like the fish bone, both gratingly painful and downright dangerous.

Dash didn't love Savannah. He refused to allow himself to wallow in the emotion a second time. He was attracted to her the way any other red-blooded male would be. But love was out of the question. Denise had taught him everything he needed to know about that weak and destructive emotion.

He hadn't thought about Denise, except in passing, in years. Briefly he wondered if she was happy, and doubted it was possible for his ex-wife to find whatever it was in life she was searching for so desperately. He'd been a fool over his ex-wife. Her unfaithfulness continued to haunt him even now, years after their divorce. He'd turned a blind eye to her faults, all in the glorious name of love.

He'd made mistakes too, Dash realized. First and foremost he had married the wrong woman. His father had tried to tell him, but Dash had refused to listen, discrediting his parent's advice, confident his father's qualms about Dash's choice in women were part and parcel of being too old to understand true love. Time had proved otherwise.

Looking back, Dash realized he shared only one thing with Denise. Incredible sex. He'd mistaken her physical demands on him for love. Within a few weeks of their meeting they were living together and their frequent bouts of sex had become addictive.

It was ironic that she'd been the one who brought up the subject of marriage. Until then she'd insisted she was a free spirit. Not until much later did he understand this sudden need she had for commitment. Dash was due to graduate soon and with his father deathly ill, there was the possibility of a large inheritance.

They'd been happy in the beginning. Dash attempted to convince himself of that, and perhaps they were, but their happiness was shockingly short-lived.

He first suspected something was awry when he arrived home late one evening after a grueling day in court and thought he caught the scent of a man's cologne. He asked Denise and she assured him he was imagining things. Because he wanted to believe her, because the thought of her being unfaithful was so completely foreign, he'd accepted her word. He had no reason to doubt her.

His second clue came less than a month later when a woman he didn't know met him outside his apartment. She was petite and fragile in her full-length coat, her hands buried deep in the pockets, her eyes downcast. She hated to trouble him, she said, but could Dash please keep his wife away from her husband. She'd recently learned she was pregnant with their second child and wanted to hold the marriage together if she could.

Dash had been stunned. He'd tried to ask questions, but she'd turned and fled. He didn't say anything to Denise, not that night and not for a long time afterward. It was only then that he started to notice the little things that should have been obvious.

Dash hated himself for being so weak. He should have demanded the truth then and there, should have kicked her out of his home. Instead he did nothing. Nothing. Denial was comfortable for a week and then two while he wrestled with his doubts.

Savannah's scarred leg was a testament to her bravery, her endless struggle to face life each and every day. His scarred emotions were a testament to his cowardice, to knowing that his wife was cheating on him and accepting it rather than confronting her with the truth.

His wife had been *cheating* on him. What an ineffectual word that was for what he felt. The sense of betrayal was sharper than any blade, more painful than any incision. It carved out his ego, punctured his heart and forever changed the way he viewed love and life.

Dash had loved Denise; he must have, otherwise she wouldn't have held the power to hurt him so deeply. That love, that emotion that had burned within him, slowly twisted itself into a bitter desire to get even.

The divorce had been ugly. Dash attempted to use legal means for what Denise had done to him emotionally. Unfortunately there was no compensation for what he'd endured. He'd learned this countless times since from other clients. He'd wanted to embarrass and humiliate her the way she had him, but in the end they were both losers.

Following their divorce, Denise had married again almost immediately, to a man she'd met three weeks earlier. Dash kept tabs on her for a year or so afterward, and was downright gleeful when he learned she was divorcing again some time later.

For a long while Dash was convinced he hated Denise. In some ways he did; his need for revenge was childlike and immature. But as the years passed, he was able to put some perspective into their short marriage and he was grateful for the valuable lessons she'd taught him. Paramount was the complete worthlessness of love and marriage.

Denise had initiated him into this school of thinking and the hundreds of divorce cases he'd handled since then had reinforced his low opinion of love and marriage.

Then he'd met Savannah. In the beginning, she'd irritated him no end. With her head in the clouds, subsisting on the whimsically thin air of romance, she'd met each of his arguments as if she alone were responsible for defending the institution of marriage. As if she alone were responsible for changing his views.

Savannah irritated him—that was true enough—but gradually she'd worn down his defenses until he was doing more than listening to her; he was beginning to believe again. It took some deep soul-searching to admit that.

He must believe, otherwise she wouldn't be sleeping in his bed. Otherwise they wouldn't have come within a heartbeat of making love.

What a drastic mistake that would have been, Dash realized a second time, grateful for the sudden turn of events. He didn't know when common sense had abandoned him, but it had. Perhaps he'd taken to breathing that impossibly thin air Savannah had existed on all these years. It had apparently tricked him as it had her.

Dash should have known better than to bring Savannah into his home. He couldn't sleep with her and expect their relationship to remain the same. Everything would change. Savannah wasn't the type of woman to engage in casual affairs and that was all Dash had to offer. A few hours together in bed would have been immensely pleasurable, but eventually disastrous to them both.

There must have been something more in the champagne they'd drunk. Warning lights should have been flashing, bells should have been ringing a long time before now.

She'd tasted so damn sweet and eager in his arms. Her willingness had gone straight to his head like a shot of ninety-proof moonshine. All he could think about was getting her home and making love to her. All he could think about was wrapping her legs around his waist and relieving the sexual frustration that had been building in him from the first moment they'd kissed all those weeks ago.

It was insanity at the highest level. He didn't know what the hell was wrong with him.

Savannah woke when dawn crept over the horizon. Opening her eyes, it took her a moment to orient herself. She was in a strange bed. Alone. Her mind moved at laser speed in an effort to remember the events from the night before. It didn't take half a second to put everything back into perspective and remember she was in Dash's home.

Sitting up proved to be something of a chore, rushing as she was. The contents of her purse were strewn across the top of the mattress and, gathering them together as quickly as possible, she went in search of her shoes.

Dash was nowhere to be seen, and if her luck held, she could call for a cab and be out of his home before he realized she'd gone.

The weight of her folly felt like she was hauling around blocks of concrete. She'd never felt more embarrassed in her life.

She moved silently from the bedroom into the living room. Pausing, she found Dash asleep in his recliner. Her breath caught in her throat as she whispered a silent prayer of thanksgiving that he was sound asleep.

Fearing the slightest sound would wake Dash, she decided to sneak out the back door, find a phone elsewhere and call for a cab.

Her hand was on the lock to the back door, a clean escape within her reach, when Dash spoke from behind her.

"I thought you wanted to check out my china pattern."

Savannah closed her eyes in abject frustration. "You were sleeping," she said without turning around.

"I'm awake now."

The heat in her face was so hot, it was painful. Dropping her hands, she did her best to put on a smile, before slowly pivoting around to face him.

"How were you planning on getting home?" he asked.

"A taxi."

"Do you carry a phone with you?"

He knew perfectly well she didn't. "No, I was going to locate a public phone and call for one there."

"I see." He began to assemble a pot of coffee as if this morning were no different than any other. "Why did you find it so important to leave now?" he demanded in what she was sure were deceptively calm tones.

"You were sleeping...."

"And you didn't want to disturb me," he supplied.

"Something like that."

"We didn't make love, so there's no need to behave like the outraged virgin."

"I'm well aware of what we did and didn't do," Savannah said stiffly. He was offended that she was sneaking out of his home. That much was apparent in the steel line of his jaw. A muscle jerked there, spelling out his dissatisfaction with her. He should be accustomed to that by now. She'd proven to be more than unsatisfactory.

Dash was an experienced lover, but she doubted that he'd ever dealt with a situation similar to what had happened to them. Most women probably found pleasure in his touch, not excruciating pain. Most women sighed with enjoyment, *not* sobbed in agony. Most women lived the life of a princess on a day-to-day basis, while her opportunity came once in a lifetime.

"How's your leg feel?"

"It's fine."

"You shouldn't have danced...."

"Nothing on this earth would have stopped me," she told him, her voice surprisingly strong. "The pain was something I live with every day. It didn't come as a surprise. It was the price I paid for enjoying myself. I had a wonderful time last night, Dash. Don't take that away from me."

He hesitated, then said, "Sit down and have a cup of coffee. We'll talk and then I'll drive you home." He poured two cups of the steaming brew and set them on the round kitchen table.

"I... I'm not much of a conversationalist in the morning."

"No problem. We can wait until afternoon if you'd rather."

She didn't and he knew that. All she wanted was to escape, to crawl into a hole and lick her wounds.

Reluctantly she pulled out the chair and sat down. The coffee was too hot to drink, but just the right temperature for the ceramic cup to warm her hands. She cradled it between her palms and focused her attention on it. "I want you to know how sorry I am for—"

"If you're making an apology for what happened last night, I suggest you don't," he interrupted.

"All right, I won't."

"Good."

Savannah took her first tentative sip of coffee. "Well," she said, looking up but avoiding his eyes, "what would you suggest we talk about?"

"What happened."

"Nothing happened."

"It damn near did."

"I know that better than you think, Dash. So why are we acting like strangers this morning? Susan's wedding was a beautiful experience. Dancing with you and the two elderly gentlemen from your office was wonderful. For one incredible night I played the glamorous role of a princess. Unfortunately, it ended just a little too soon."

"It ended exactly where it should have. Our making love would have been a mistake."

Savannah was trying to put everything in proper perspective, but for him to come right out and tell her he was relieved they hadn't made love felt like a slap in the face. It shouldn't have hurt so much, but it did. Unwanted tears sprang to her eyes.

"You don't agree?"

"It doesn't matter if I do or don't, does it?" she asked, not wanting him to know how deeply he'd hurt her. She didn't blame him. No man wanted to make love to a cripple. Men wanted women who were whole and healthy to share their bed.

"I suppose it doesn't matter."

"It doesn't," she said more forcefully. She was having a difficult time holding back the tears that burned just beneath the surface. They threatened to brim and spill down her face at any moment. "I'd like to go home now," she said.

"It wouldn't have worked, you know."

"Of course I know that," she flared.

She felt more than saw Dash's hesitation. "Are you all right?"

"I've never been better," she snapped. "But I want to go home. Sitting around here in this dress is ridiculous. Now either you drive me or I'm calling a cab."

He didn't need a long time to make up his mind. "I'll drive you."

The ride back to her home was a nightmare for Savannah. Dash made a couple of attempts at conversation, but she was in no mood to talk and certainly in no mood to dissect the events of the night before. She'd been humiliated enough and wasn't looking to make matters worse.

The minute Dash pulled into her driveway, Savannah's hand was on the car door, eager and ready to make her escape. His hand at her elbow stopped her.

Savannah groaned inwardly and froze. Unfortunately, Dash didn't seem to have anything to say.

"Susan's wedding was very nice. Thank you," he told her finally.

She nodded, keeping her back to him and her head lowered.

"I enjoyed our time together."

"I . . . did, too." But then, a princess generally did. It was only when she returned to the disfigured woman that the magic disappeared.

"I'll give you a call later in the week."

She nodded, although she didn't believe it. This was probably a line he used often. It sounded trite and stale, as if he'd said it to any number of women.

"What about Thursday?" he asked unexpectedly, after he'd helped her out of the car.

"What about it?"

"I'd like to take you out.... A picnic or something."

He couldn't have surprised her more. Slowly she raised her head, her eyes studying him, confident she'd misunderstood him.

He met her gaze steadily. "Is something wrong?"

"Are you asking me out on a date?"

"Yes," he said, taking her house keys out of her lifeless hand and unlocking her front door for her. "Is that a problem?"

"I...I don't know."

"Would you prefer it if we went dancing instead?" he asked, his mouth lifting in a half smile.

Despite their terrible beginning that morning, Savannah smiled. "It'd be nice, but I think not."

"I'll see what I can arrange. I'll pick you up around six at the shop. Is that all right?"

Savannah was too shocked to do anything but nod.

"Good." With that he cupped her shoulders, leaned forward and brushed his lips over hers. It wasn't much as kisses go, but the warmth of his touch went through her like a bolt of lightning.

Savannah stood on her porch, watching him walk away. He was at his car before he turned back. He held open the driver's door. "You made a beautiful princess."

* * *

Dash wasn't sure what prompted the invitation for a picnic for Thursday. It wasn't something he'd given any thought to suggesting. In fact, he was as surprised as Savannah looked when he'd asked her.

A date. It was a simple enough thing. It wasn't as if he hadn't gone out on a date before, but it had been a good long while since he'd formally asked a woman out. He was making more of this than necessary, he decided.

By Wednesday he would have welcomed an excuse to get out of the agreed meeting. Especially after John Stackhouse called Dash into his office. The minute he received the summons, Dash guessed this was somehow linked to Savannah.

"You wanted to see me?" Dash asked, stepping inside the senior partner's office later that afternoon.

"I hope I'm not calling you away from something important?"

"Not at all," Dash assured him. It might have been his imagination, but it seemed Stackhouse's attitude was decidedly friendly. Generally the two were stiffly polite to each other. Paul Justice seemed to have a good working relationship with the older man, not Dash. But then, Paul wasn't prone to disagree with anyone who was in a position of advancing his career.

"I have a divorce case I want you to handle," his boss said casually.

These cases were often assigned to him. He'd built his reputation on them, cut his eye teeth on his own. Of late, they hadn't held his interest and he was hoping to diversify.

"This man is a friend of mine by the name of Don Griffin. This is a sad case, very sad." John paused and wiped a hand down the side of his face.

"Don Griffin," Dash repeated, finding the name familiar and not able to place where he knew it from.

"You might have heard of him. Don owns a chain of seafood restaurants throughout the Pacific Northwest."

"I think I remember reading something about him not long ago."

"You might have," John agreed. "He's mentioned in the paper every now and again. Now, getting back to the unfortunate news of the divorce.... Don and Janice have been married a good many years. They have two college-age children and then Janice learned a few years back that she was pregnant. You can imagine their shock."

Dash nodded.

"Unfortunately the child is retarded. This came as a second blow and Don took it hard, but then, so did Janice."

Dash couldn't blame the couple for that. "They're divorcing?"

John Stackhouse's nod was filled with regret. "I don't know all the details, but apparently Janice was devoting all her time and attention to little Amy and well, in a moment of weakness, Don became involved with another woman. Janice found out about it and filed for divorce."

"I see. And is this what Don wants?"

The senior partner's face tightened with disappointment. "Apparently so. I'm asking you as a personal favor to me if you'd handle this case on my behalf, representing Don. My late wife and I were good friends with both Don and Janice."

"I'd be happy to help in any way I could," Dash said, but without any real enthusiasm. Another divorce case, lives stripped apart. He'd anesthetize his feelings as best he could and struggle to work out the necessary details, but only because John had asked him.

"I'll make an appointment for Don to come in for the initial consultation Friday morning, if that's agreeable?" Once more he made it a question, as if he expected Dash to decline.

Dash hesitated, not knowing how to proceed. This was the first personal favor Stackhouse had ever asked of him.

"I'll be happy to take the case," Dash said finally.

"Good," John said, reaching for his phone. "I'll let Don know I've gotten him the best divorce attorney in town."

"Thank you." Compliments were few and far between with the eldest of the senior partners. Dash suspected he should be encouraged that the older man trusted him with good family friends.

On his way out of the office, Dash ran into Arnold Sterle. "Dash," the other man said, his face lighting up with a bright smile. "I haven't seen you all week."

"I've been in court."

"So I heard. I just wanted you to know how much I enjoyed attending your sister's wedding."

"We enjoyed having you." So he wasn't going to escape hearing about Savannah after all.

"How's Savannah?" Arnold asked eagerly.

"Very well. I'll tell her you asked about her."

"Please do. My granddaughter's thinking about getting married. I'd like to steer her to Savannah's shop. If your sister's wedding is evidence of the kind of work Savannah does, I'd like to hire her myself." He chuckled then. "Not that I have much say in these affairs. If you could, have Savannah mail me a few brochures."

"I'll do that."

"I sincerely hope you appreciate what a special woman she is."

"I do."

"Good," Arnold said, grinning broadly. "I'm very pleased to hear that."

By Thursday evening, Dash had run the full gauntlet of mixed emotions. Knowing he'd be seeing Savannah later was a curse and a blessing. He looked forward to being with her and at the same time dreaded it. To claim he was confused was putting it mildly.

He arrived right on time. Savannah was sitting at her desk, and apparently she didn't hear him enter the shop because she didn't look up. She was probably entertaining second thoughts of her own.

"Savannah." He said her name lightly, not wanting to frighten her.

She jerked her head up then, surprise written on her face. It wasn't the shock he read in her eyes that unnerved him, it was the tears.

"What are you doing here?" she demanded.

"It's Thursday. We have a date. Remember?"

It seemed to Dash she had forgotten.

"Are you going to tell me what's upset you so much?" he asked.

"No," she said with a warm smile, the welcome in her eyes discounting her distress. "I'm pleased to see you, Dash, really pleased. I could do with a friend just now."

Chapter Eight

Savannah hadn't forgotten about her date with Dash. She'd thought of little else in the preceding days, wondering if she should put any credence to his asking. One thing she knew about Dash Davenport, he wasn't the type to suggest something he didn't want.

"I had the deli pack us dinner," he told her. "From the look of the basket, I sincerely hope you're hungry."

"I am," she assured him, wiping the last remnant of tears from her face. Dash was studying her with undisguised curiosity and she was grateful he didn't press her for details. She wouldn't have known how to explain, wouldn't have found the words to tell him the sadness and guilt she carried with her today. Savannah had accepted the fact she would never be like others. When she was a girl she used to close her eyes and dream of all the things she longed to do. Foremost on her list was to fly. She yearned to soar above her problems, fly free of yesterday's guilt and tomorrow's fears. As she matured, she came to realize more and more how impossible that would be.

"Where are we going?" she asked, locking up the shop. If ever there was a time she needed to get away, to abandon her woes and have fun, it was now.

"Lake Sammamish."

The large lake east of Lake Washington was a well-known and well-loved picnic area. Savannah had visited there several times over the years, mostly in the autumn, when she stopped by to admire the spectacular display of fall colors. She enjoyed walking along the shore and feeding the ducks.

"I brought along a change of clothes," she explained. "It'll only take me a minute to get out of this suit."

"Don't rush. We aren't in any hurry."

Savannah moved into the dressing room and replaced her business outfit with jeans and a large sweatshirt embossed with Einstein's image. She'd purchased it earlier in the week with this outing in mind. When she returned, she discovered Dash examining a posh silk wedding dress adorned with a pearl yoke. She smiled to herself, remembering the first time he'd entered her shop and the way he'd avoided getting close to anything that hinted of romance. He'd come a long way in the past few months, farther than he realized, much farther than she'd expected.

"This gown arrived from New York this afternoon. It's lovely, isn't it?"

She expected him to shrug and back away, embarrassed that she'd commented on his noticing something as symbolic of love as a wedding dress.

"It's beautiful. Did one of your clients order it?"

"Not exactly. It's from a designer I've worked with in the past and I fell in love with it myself. I do that every once in a while...order a dress that appeals to me personally. Generally they sell, and if they don't, there's always the possibility of renting it out."

"Not this one," he said in a voice so low, she had to strain to hear him. He seemed mesmerized by the dress.

"Why not?" she asked.

"This is the type of wedding gown..." He hesitated.

"Yes?" she prompted.

"When a man sees the woman he loves wearing this dress, he'll cherish the memory."

Savannah couldn't believe what she was hearing. This was Dash? The man who'd ranted and raved that love was a wasted emotion? The man who claimed marriage was for the weak and the sick?

"What a romantic thing to say," Savannah murmured. "If you don't object, I'd like to advertise it that way." Dash's eyes widened and he shook his head as if needing to clear his head. "You want to use that for an advertisement?"

"If you don't object. I won't mention your name, if you'd rather I didn't."

"No. I mean... Can we just drop this?"

"Of course. I'm sorry, I didn't mean to embarrass you."

"You didn't," he said stiffly, when it was clear she had. "I seem to have done this to myself." He made a point of looking at his watch, eager to be on his way. "Are you ready?"

Savannah nodded. This could prove to be an interesting picnic after all.

They drove to Lake Sammamish in Dash's car and he seemed extra talkative. "Arnold Sterle asked about you the other day," he told her as he wove in and out of traffic, which was especially heavy heading for the east side.

"He's a dear," Savannah said, savoring the memories of the two older men who'd worked so hard to bolster her self-confidence, vying for her the way they had. "Mr. Stackhouse, too," she added.

"You certainly made an impression on those two."

A princess would, she reminded herself. Although the night had ended in disaster, she would always treasure dancing with Dash. Without knowing what he'd done, he'd gifted her with a precious jewel.

"What's the smile all about?" Dash asked, momentarily taking his eyes off the road.

"It's nothing."

"The tears were nothing, too?"

The tears. She'd almost forgotten she'd been crying when he first arrived. "I was talking to my parents this afternoon," she said as the misery returned full force. "It's always the same. They talk about traveling, but they never seem to leave Seattle. Instead of really enjoying their life they smother me with their sympathy and their sacrifices, as if that were enough to bring back the full use of my leg." She was speaking so fast and furiously that the words ran into each other. Not until she'd finished did she realize how close she was to weeping again.

Dash's hand closed around hers. He remembered now what Savannah had told him about her parents' reaction to the accident. He hadn't realized how difficult it was for her.

"You're a mature adult, living independently of them. You have for years."

"Which I've explained so many times, I get angry just thinking about it. Apparently they feel if something were to happen to me, no one would be here to take care of me."

"What about other relatives?"

"There aren't any in the Seattle area. I try to reassure them that I'm fine, that no disasters are about to strike and even if one did, I have plenty of close friends to call on, but they just won't leave."

"What was it that upset you this afternoon?" Dash prompted.

Savannah dropped her gaze to her hands clenched tightly in her lap. "They've decided to remain in Seattle this winter. Good friends of theirs asked them to travel with them, leaving the second week of September and touring the South before spending the winter in Arizona. My dad has always wanted to visit New Orleans and Atlanta. They decided to go another year," Savannah said, "but I know they won't. They know it, too."

Once again Dash didn't speak for a couple of moments. "Your parents love you. I can understand their concerns."

"How can you say that?" she demanded angrily. "They're doing this because they feel guilty about my accident. Now I'm the one who's carrying that load. When will it ever end?"

"I don't know," Dash admitted.

"I just wish they loved me enough to trust me to take care of myself. I've been doing exactly that for a long time now."

"I know." Dash exited from the freeway and took the road leading into Lake Sammamish State Park. He drove around until he found a picnic table located close to the parking lot. The gesture was a thoughtful one; he didn't want her to have a long way to walk.

He wasn't being very subtle, but Savannah didn't care. She was determined to enjoy this outing. She needed this. Needing someone was alien to her. It was dangerous to allow herself this luxury. She was well aware that Dash could be out of her life with little notice. She'd always taken that into account in other relationships, but her guard had slipped with Dash.

He helped her out of the car and carried the thick wicker basket to the bright blue picnic table. The late afternoon was filled with a symphony of pleasant sounds. Birds chirped in a nearby tree and mingled with the laughter of children. Nature seemed to hum in three-part harmony until it was like listening to soothing music from a radio.

"I'm starved," Dash announced, peeking inside one end of the basket. He raised his head and jiggled his thick eyebrows. "My, oh, my, what goodies."

Savannah spread a tablecloth across one end of the table and Dash handed her a large loaf of French bread, followed by a bottle of red wine.

"That's for show," he said, grinning broadly. "This is for dinner." With that he took out a bucket of chicken and a six-pack of soda.

"I thought you said the deli packed this," Savannah chastised.

"They did. I made a list of what I wanted and they packed it inside the basket for me."

"You're beginning to sound like a tricky defense attorney," she said, enjoying this easy banter between them. It helped take her mind off her parents and their uncomfortable conversation earlier in the afternoon.

They sat across the table from each other and with a chicken leg poised in front of her mouth, Savannah looked out over the blue-green water. The day was perfect. Not too warm and not too cool. The sun was shining and would have grown too warm if not for a gentle breeze that rippled off the lake. A lifeguard stood sentinel over a group of preschool children who teased the water, running in and out, wetting their toes between bursts of laughter. Farther out on the lake a group of teens dived off a large platform. Another group circled the waters in two-seater pedal boats, their wake disrupting the quiet serenity of the water.

"You're looking thoughtful," Dash commented.

Savannah blushed, a little embarrassed to be caught so enraptured with the scene spread out before her. "When I was a teenager I used to dream of a boy asking me to pedal one of the boats with him."

"Did anyone?"

"No...." A sadness attached itself to her heart, dredging up the memories of a difficult youth. "I can't pedal."

"Why not? You danced, didn't you?"

"Yes, but that's different."

"How's that?"

"Don't you remember what happened after the dance?" She lowered her gaze, not wanting him to see how badly she longed to do as he suggested, but she couldn't. Not without counting the price first.

"We could rent a pedal boat and I could do the work," he suggested.

"We'd go around in circles," she countered, shaking her head. She wasn't willing to try. "It doesn't work if we each don't do our own share of the pedaling. I appreciate what you're doing, but I simply can't hold up my part." Being reminded of her limitation was always difficult, but more so now. If ever there was a man she wanted to be normal for, it was Dash. It hurt to refuse him, more than it had hurt with anyone else.

"You don't know that until you try," he insisted. "Remember, you didn't want to dance, either." His reminder was a gentle one and it hit its mark well.

"We might end up looking like fools."

"So? It's happened before." He stood and offered her his hand. "You game or not?"

She stared up at him, and indecision kept her rooted to the table. "I don't know if this is such a good idea."

"Come on, Savannah, prove to me that you can do this. But more important, prove it to yourself. I'm not going to let you overdo it this time, I promise."

His confidence was contagious. "If you're insinuating that you could have kept me off the dance floor, think again, big boy. I danced every dance."

"Don't remind me. The only way I could be with you was to cut in on someone else. At least this way I'll have you to myself."

Savannah placed her hand firmly in his, caught up in the rapture of his smile.

"If anyone else comes seeking the pleasure of your company this time," he said, "they'll have to swim."

Savannah's mood had been painfully introspective when Dash first arrived. Now, for the first time in what seemed like days, she experienced the overwhelming need to laugh. Hugging Dash was a spontaneous reaction to the lighthearted feeling being with him lent her.

He stiffened when her arms first went around him, but recovered quickly, gripping her about her waist, lifting her and twirling her around until she had to beg him to stop. Breathless, she gazed up at him, and said, "You make me want to sing."

"You make me want to—" He stopped abruptly.

"What?" she asked.

"Sing," he muttered, relaxing his hold enough for her feet to touch the ground.

Savannah could have sworn his ears turned red, which was something she didn't understand. "I make you want to do what?" she pressed.

"Never mind, Savannah," he answered from between clenched teeth. "It's better that you don't know. And please, just for this one time, is it too much to ask that you don't argue with me?"

"If you insist," she said, pretending to be gravely disappointed. She mocked him with a deep sigh that deflated her shoulders.

They walked down to the water's edge, where Dash paid for the rental of the two-seater pedal boat. He helped her to board and then joined her, the boat rocking precariously as he shifted his weight.

Savannah held tightly on to her seat. She remained skeptical of this idea, convinced they were going to look like a pair of idiots once they made their way from shore. She didn't mind being laughed at, but she wasn't confident Dash would feel the same way.

"I...don't think we should do this," she whispered. Her fingers were biting into the hard flesh of his upper arm as an attack of cowardice struck her.

"I'm not letting you out of this now. We haven't even tried."

"I'll embarrass you."

"Let me worry about that."

"Dash, please."

He refused to listen to her and began working the bicyclelike pedals with a gentle eagerness, being sure the pace he set wasn't too much for her. Water rustled from behind them and Savannah jerked around to see the paddle wheel churning up the water. Before she realized it, they were moving at a fast clip.

"We're moving," she shouted. "We're actually moving."

It seemed everyone on the shore turned to watch them. In a display of sheer delight, Savannah waved her arms. "We're actually moving."

"I think they've got the general idea," Dash teased.

"I could just kiss you," Savannah said, resisting the urge to loop her arms around his neck and do exactly that.

"If you wait a few moments, I'll let you." His hand reached for hers and he entwined their fingers.

"Let's go fast," she urged, pumping her feet with all her might. "I want to see how fast we can go."

"Savannah...no."

"Yes, please, just for a little bit."

He groaned and then complied. The blades of the paddle behind them churned up the water into a frothy texture as they sped ahead. Dash was doing the majority of the work. Her efforts were puny compared to his, but it didn't seem to matter. This was more fun than she'd dared to dream. At least as much fun as dancing.

Savannah threw back her head and laughed boisterously. "I never knew," she said, squeezing his upper arm with both hands and pressing her head against his shoulder. "I never thought I could do this."

"There's a whole world out there just waiting to be explored."

"I want to sky dive next," Savannah offered gleefully.

"Sky dive?"

"All right, roller-skate. I longed to so badly when I was growing up. I used to skate before the accident, you know. I was pretty good, too."

"I'm sure you were."

"All my life I've felt hindered because of my disability and all of a sudden a whole new world of possibilities is opening up to me." She went from one emotional extreme to the other. First joy and laughter and now tears and sadness. "Meeting you was the best thing that's ever happened to me," she said, and sniffled. "I could cry, I'm so happy."

Dash stiffened and Savannah wondered if she'd offended him. His reaction would have been imperceptible if they hadn't been sitting side by side, her thigh pressing against his. Her side butting against his own, her shoulder rubbing his.

Dash was pedaling harder now; her own feet were carried with the action, although she wasn't adding much pressure. "Where are we going?" she asked, noting that he seemed to be steering the craft toward the shore. She didn't want to stop, not when they were just getting started. This was her one fear, that she'd embarrass him, and apparently she had.

"See that weeping-willow tree over on the far side of the bank?" he asked, motioning down the shore-line. She did, noting the lush growth that edged out over the water like a sanctuary. It appeared to be on private property.

"Yes."

"We're headed there."

"But why?" she asked, thinking of any number of plausible reasons. Perhaps he knew the people who lived there and wanted to stop and say hello. Maybe he wanted to leave her and return for her later.

"Because that weeping willow offers a tad more privacy than out here on the lake. And I intend to take you up on your offer, because frankly, I'm not going to be able to wait much longer."

Offer, she mused. What offer?

Dash seemed to enjoy her dilemma and raised her hand to his mouth, kissing the inside of her palm. "I seem to remember you claiming you wanted to kiss me. I'm giving you the opportunity to do exactly that."

"Now?"

"In a moment." He steered the boat into the drooping, spindly arms of the tree. Spiny fingers dipped into the water. The dense growth cut off the sunlight and cooled the late-afternoon air.

Dash stopped and the boat settled, motionless, in the water. He turned to her and his gaze slid like silk across her face.

"Has anyone ever told you how beautiful you are?"

No one. Not ever. "No."

"Is the rest of the world blind?"

His words were followed by silence. A silence that had spanned years for Savannah. A silence that echoed in the darkest chambers of her soul. No man had whispered sweet nothings to her. No man had looked past her flaw and seen the desirable woman she longed to be. No man but Dash.

His mouth came down on hers, shattering the silence with his hungry need, shattering the self-imposed discipline she'd held herself under all these years. She wrapped herself in his embrace and returned the kiss with the potency of her own need.

Dash moaned and kissed her hard and fast, and she responded with every ounce of her being. She kissed him as if she'd been waiting all her life for this moment, for this man. In ways too numerous to count, she had been.

His tongue danced with hers as his fingers worked their way into her thick hair. With his thumbs anchoring her cheekbones, he held her against him. His mouth nipped at hers as he lowered his hand to the pulse hammering wildly at the base of her throat. She felt the pad of his thumb pressed there and her own savage heartbeat.

Her breasts were flattened against his wide chest. She felt his strength, needed it herself.

She moaned softly, thinking nothing seemed enough. Dash made her greedy. She wanted more. More of life. More of laughter. More of him.

Dragging his mouth from hers, he trailed a row of moist kisses down her neck. "If we were anyplace but here, do you know what we'd be doing now?"

"I . . . I think so." How odd her voice sounded, as if coming from the bottom of a deep well.

"We'd be in bed making love."

"I . . ."

"What?" he prompted. "Were you about to tell me you can't? Because I'll be more than happy to prove otherwise." He directed her mouth back to his and effectively showed her with his tongue what he yearned to do with his body. Slowly, reluctantly, as though remembering this was a public place and they could be interrupted any moment, he ended the kiss, tempering it with gentleness.

Savannah had more of a problem than Dash returning to sanity. He was warm and hard and she needed the solid reality of him close to her. When he eased himself from her arms, his eyes searched out hers. His were soft, giving, gentle. Savannah guessed that hers were those things, too, but beneath the veneer she was confused and uncertain.

"If you say that shouldn't have happened, I swear I'll do something crazy," she whispered.

"I don't think I could make myself say it."

"Good," she breathed.

Dash pressed his forehead to hers. "Damn, but I wish I knew what it was you do to me." It troubled him that she could break through that facade of his and make him want her so desperately. She was beginning to understand this man. She was physically handicapped, but Dash was crippled, too. He didn't want love, but he couldn't keep himself from caring about her and that worried him. It worried her, too.

"You don't like what I do to you, do you?" That much was obvious, but she wanted to hear him admit it.

Dash made a short, cackling laugh. "That's the problem, I like it too damn much. There's never been anyone who affects me the way you do. Not since Denise."

"Your ex-wife?"

"Yes." He regretted mentioning her name, Savannah guessed, because he made a point of changing the subject immediately afterward.

"It's time we went back."

"Not yet," Savannah pleaded. "Not so soon. We just got started."

"I don't want you to strain your leg. You aren't accustomed to this much exercise."

"I won't, I promise. Just a little while longer." This was such glorious fun, she didn't want it to ever end. It wasn't every day that she could turn a dream into reality. It wasn't every day a man kissed her as if she were his cherished love.

Love. Love. Love. The word repeated itself in her mind like a ricocheting bullet. She was falling in love with Dash. It had started weeks earlier, the first time he'd kissed her, and had been growing little by little each day since. Love was a dangerous emotion when it came to Dash. He wouldn't be an easy man to care about.

He steered them out of the limbs of the tree and into the sunlight. Savannah squinted against the glare, but it didn't seem to affect Dash. He pedaled now as if he was escaping something. The fun was gone.

"I'm ready to go back," Savannah said after several minutes of grating silence.

"Good." He didn't bother to disguise his relief.

The mood had changed so abruptly that Savannah had trouble taking it all in. Dash couldn't seem to get back to shore fast enough. He helped her out of the boat and placed his arm, grudgingly it seemed, around her waist to be certain she was on steady legs. Once he was confident she had her balance, he released her.

"I think we should leave," he said when they returned to the picnic table.

"Sure," she agreed, disappointed and sad. She folded up the tablecloth and handed it to him. He carried the basket to the car and loaded it in the trunk.

Savannah knew what was coming; she'd been through it countless times before. Whenever a man feared he was becoming emotionally attached to her, she could count on the same speech. Generally it began with what an exceptional woman she was, talented, gifted, fun, that sort of thing. The conclusion, however, was always the same. Someday a special man would come into her life. The promise of someday was dangled before her like the proverbial carrot. She'd never expected her relationship with Dash to get that far. She'd never expected to see him after Susan's wedding. This outing was an unforeseen bonus.

They were on the freeway, driving toward Seattle, before Savannah had enough courage to speak. It would help matters considerably if she broached the subject first.

"Thank you, Dash, for a lovely picnic."

He said nothing, which was just as well.

"I know what you're thinking," she said, gripping her hands tightly together.

"I doubt that."

She smiled to herself. "I've seen this happen with other men, so you don't need to worry about it."

"Worry about what?"

"You're attracted to me and that frightens you, probably you more than the other men I've dated because a woman you once loved has deeply hurt you."

"I said I don't want to talk about Denise."

"I'm not going to ask you about her, if that's what concerns you," she said quickly, wanting to relieve his mind of that. "I'm going to talk about us. You may not realize it now, but I'm saving you the trouble of searching for the right words."

He jerked his head away from traffic and glared at her. "I beg your pardon."

"You heard me right. You see, it's all familiar, so you needn't worry about it. This isn't the first time."

"It isn't?" The question was heavy with sarcasm.

"I've already explained this has happened before."

"Go on. I'd be interested in hearing this." The hard muscles of his face relaxed and the beginnings of a smile came into play, working at the edges of his mouth and the corners of his eyes.

"You like me."

"That much should be fairly obvious," he commented.

"I like you, too."

"That's a comfort." The sarcastic edge was back, but it wasn't biting.

"In fact, you're beginning to like me a little too much."

"I'm not sure what that means, but go on."

"We nearly made love once."

"Twice," he corrected. "We were closer than you think a few minutes ago."

"Under a tree in a pedal boat?" she asked with a laugh.

"Trust me, honey, where there's a will, there's a way."

Savannah blushed and looked pointedly away. "Let's not get sidetracked."

"Good idea."

He was flustering her, distracting her train of thought. "It becomes a bit uncomfortable whenever a man finds me attractive."

"Why's that?"

"Because...well, because they have to deal with my impediment, and most people are more comfortable ignoring it. If you deny that something's different, it just might go away."

"Have I done that?" The question was more serious than the others.

"No," she admitted grudgingly. "You've been accepting of my handicap. I'm just not sure—"

"I've never viewed you as handicapped," he interrupted.

It seemed important to him that she acknowledge that, so she did. "I'm grateful to have met you, Dash, grateful for the fun times we've shared."

"This is beginning to sound like a brush-off."

"It is," she admitted reluctantly. "I'm saving you the trouble of coming up with an excuse for not seeing me again. This is the better-to-be-honest-now-instead-of-cruel-later scenario."

"Saving me the trouble," he exploded, and then burst into gales of laughter. "So that's what this is all about."

"Yes. You can't tell me that isn't what you were thinking. I know the signs, Dash. Things got a bit heavy between us and now you're getting cold feet. It happened the night of Susan's wedding, too. We didn't make love and you were grateful, remember?"

He didn't agree or disagree.

"Just now...at the lake, we kissed, and you could feel it happening a second time, and that's dangerous. You couldn't get away from me fast enough."

"That's not entirely true."

"Your mood certainly changed."

"Okay, I'll concede that, but not for the reasons you're assuming. My mood changed because I started thinking about something and frankly it threw me for a loop."

"Thinking about what?" she pressed.

"A solution."

"To what?" Even now he seemed entirely too close lipped.

"Hold on, Savannah, because I don't know how you're going to react. Probably about the same way I did."

"Go on," she urged.

"It seemed to me . . ."

"Yes?" she urged when he didn't immediately finish.

"It seems to me that we might want to think about getting married."

Chapter Nine

"**M**arried," Savannah repeated in a husky whisper.

Dash knew he'd shocked her, but no more so than he had himself. Entertaining the notion of them marrying went against the very grain of his consciousness. Something was either very wrong, or very right. He had yet to decide.

"I don't understand," Savannah said, making an aimless flip-flop gesture with her hands.

"Unfortunately, I don't know that I'll do a decent job of explaining it," Dash admitted reluctantly.

"Try," she suggested. Her hands were at her throat now, fingering the collar of her sweatshirt. The very one he'd considered stripping from her on the lake, so he could taste her breasts and bury his face in the fullness of her bounty.

"This could work, Savannah, with a little effort on both our parts."

"You hate the very word. . . . I've never met anyone with a more jaded attitude toward love and romance. Is this some kind of a joke?"

"Trust me. I'm just as shocked at the idea as you, but the more I thought about it, the more sense it made. I wish it were a joke." Dash's choice of words must have been poor because Savannah recoiled from him so fast, he feared she might have damaged her neck. "It would be a marriage of convenience," he added, hoping that would calm her sensitivities.

"What?" she cried. "In other words, you intend to take what I consider sacred and make a mockery of it."

It was difficult not to be defensive when Savannah was being this unreasonable. "If you'll listen, you might see there are advantages to this idea for both of us."

"Take me back to my shop," she said in a icy voice.

"I'm headed there now, but I was hoping we could talk first."

She said nothing, which didn't bode well. Dash wanted to explain, ease her mind, ease his own, but he wasn't sure he could. He'd spoken prematurely without giving the matter the serious consideration it deserved. It was after they'd kissed under the weeping-willow tree that the idea had taken root in his mind. It had boggled him so completely that for a time he could barely function. He needed to escape and now that they were on their way back into Seattle, he realized how important it was to completely talk this out with her. Apparently his timing was a bit off.

"I know this comes as a surprise," he said, looking for a means of broaching the subject once again. He exited from the freeway and was within a mile of Savannah's shop.

Savannah looked steadfastly out the window, as if the sights of the sidewalks mesmerized her.

"Say something," Dash demanded. He eased into the wide alley where her car was parked and turned off the engine. He kept his hands tightly on the steering wheel in an effort to ground himself.

"You wouldn't want to hear what I'm thinking," Savannah told him.

"Maybe not," he agreed. "But would you at least listen to what I have to say?"

She crossed her arms over her chest and glared at him with eyes so cutting, they could have sliced through concrete. "I don't know that I can and keep a straight face."

"Try," he urged, using her own terminology.

"All right, go on, explain." She closed her eyes as if she needed to block him out.

"When I came to pick you up this afternoon, you were upset. Right?"

She shrugged, unwilling to grant him even that much. It wasn't an encouraging sign. It was premature for him to have mentioned marriage. He wasn't sure why he considered it so urgent that he couldn't take the night to sleep on it first. Perhaps he was afraid he'd change his mind. Perhaps this was what he'd always wanted, and needed to cloak his pride with the marriage-of-convenience proposal. Either way, it didn't matter; he'd already exposed his hand.

"You love your parents and want them to go after the dream they've always wanted, isn't that right?"

"Would you simply make your point?"

"All right, I will," he said, his argument gaining momentum in his mind. "I'm offering you the perfect solution. We marry."

"In other words, you're suggesting we mislead my parents into believing this is a love match?"

"I hadn't thought of it in those terms, but, yes, I guess we would be misleading them. If that makes you uncomfortable, tell them the truth. Hell, you can keep your maiden name if you're so keen to do so. That wouldn't bother me. The point is, if you were married, your father and mother would feel free to move south for the winters the way they've always wanted."

"What's in this for you?" she demanded. "Don't try to tell me you're doing this out of the goodness of your heart, either. I know better."

"You're right, there're advantages to me, too."

She snickered softly. "Somehow or other I thought there would be."

"That's the beauty of this idea," he said, having something of a problem keeping his irritation in check. Savannah was treating this like some kind of joke while he was dead serious. A man didn't mention the word *marriage* lightly, even when he was crazy in love with a woman. Generally, that was the crux of the problem—he had lost his senses. Dash had been through all this before. Marriage, this time around, would be on his terms.

"Go on," Savannah urged, sounding short on patience and long on aggravating him.

"As I said, there are certain advantages in this marriage for me, as well. The night of Susan's wedding, John Stackhouse pulled me aside and told me that I was being considered for the position of senior partner."

"But it would help your case if you were married."

Savannah wasn't slow-witted, he'd give her that much. "Something like that," he admitted. "It seems the other senior partners fear that my bitterness about my divorce has spilled over into other areas of my life."

"Imagine that."

Dash's hands tightened around the steering wheel in an effort to disguise his irritation. Savannah was making this damned difficult.

"There're no guarantees for either of us, of course. If you were to agree to the terms of this marriage, that doesn't mean your parents will pack up and head south. If we were to go ahead with it, there's nothing to say I'll be made a senior partner. There's an element of risk for us both. You might get what you want and I might not."

"Ah, now I understand," Savannah said in a slow, singsong voice. "That's where this marriage of convenience comes into play. You want an out."

"That has nothing to do with it," Dash flared.

"Do you think I'm stupid, Dash? Of course it does. No one wants a cripple for a wife, and if you can put an escape clause in the marriage contract, all the better."

"Your being lame has nothing to do with this."

"And pigs fly. Would you have proposed marriage to a...normal woman this way, suggesting a short-term relationship for convenience' sake? Heaven forbid that you might feel some genuine affection for me."

"Savannah..."

"I'm crippled and therefore desperate enough to consider this . . . this insulting proposition."

It took Dash a moment to compose himself. "Maybe this wasn't such a bright idea after all. I should have ironed out the details before talking it over with you. If you want to find fault with me for that, then I'll accept it with a heartfelt apology, but this business about me using you because I consider you less of a woman—you couldn't be more wrong. Your suggestion insults us both."

"Why do I have a hard time believing that?" Savannah asked. She sounded suspiciously close to tears, which grieved him more than her anger had.

"All I'm looking for here is a means of being fair to us both," Dash argued. "Despite what you believe, I didn't mean to insult you."

"I'm sure you didn't. In your mind you're probably thinking someone will nominate you for sainthood. Imagine dashing, debonair Dashiel Davenport taking pity on that poor crippled woman. It takes a special kind of man to marry a woman with a handicap. The kind of man who would make an excellent senior partner."

"Savannah, stop." His lips were pressed so tightly together that his mouth ached. She was making a mockery of his proposal, a mockery of herself.

"Are you saying I'm wrong? Wouldn't marrying a cripple give you a slight advantage when it comes to the appointment as senior partner?"

His control was hair-thin and stretching. "Don't even suggest that," he said in biting tones.

"It's true."

Dash gritted his teeth. "Whether you choose to believe it or not, the idea I'd use you like that is unworthy of you and insulting to me."

"It's time I left," Savannah whispered. She turned from him, her fingers closing around the door handle. "It'd be best if we didn't see each other again."

Dash knew that the minute she left his car it would be over between them. He couldn't allow that to happen, couldn't let her leave, not without righting the wrong. He needed to do something, anything, to convince her he was sincere.

"Not so soon," Dash said, gripping hold of her shoulder and twisting her around so she faced him.

"Let go of me."

"Not without this." He locked his arms around her waist and dragged her flush against him. Her breasts were flattened against his chest and she was glaring at him with angry defiance, her hands clasped in tight fists. Dash reacted with his own brand of anger, his own brand of comfort as his mouth swooped down on hers.

Savannah resisted him at first, struggling, twisting her mouth back and forth, which only heightened the incredible physical need he experienced for her. He wouldn't allow his mouth to punish her, didn't dominate her with brute force, but simply let her struggle while he kissed her with a gentle tenderness. The fight in her surprised him. Her fingers tightly gripped hold of his shirtfront, bunching the material, but if she meant to strike him, her hands lost their purpose.

After a moment she whimpered and her lips parted, inviting the exploration of his tongue. That she'd learned these soft, welcoming touches of her tongue from him was a powerful aphrodisiac. He claimed several long, deep kisses that left him mindless, his judgment fogged with a need so strong, it couldn't be ignored.

His hands searched for and found her plump breasts. He unfastened her bra and groaned loudly as their generous fullness fell into his waiting palms. Her nipples were hard and hot and seemed to throb against his open hands. Tasting her became more important than breathing, but first he had to look at her. He needed to see for himself that she wanted this as badly as he did.

Savannah met his gaze with hot, angry eyes, but he noticed that she did nothing to stop him. Encouraged, he lifted the sweatshirt from her head, displaying her lush fullness for his enjoyment. Slowly he lowered his face to one of her generous breasts and gently bit the tip. She arched her back and he sucked greedily. She moaned again and again and Dash understood. This was a touch of heaven oddly tainted with a trace of hell. Glory mingled with torment.

Savannah twisted feverishly against him. He was empty and only her nourishment would fill him. He was lost and only she could show him the way. He needed her as badly as she needed him. Unfortunately, neither of them had the courage or the honesty to admit it.

Dash didn't know what brought him back to sanity. Possibly a noise from the street, or Savannah herself. He jerked his head up and buried his face against her shoulder, which was heaving with the strength of her reaction. Her fingers were buried knuckle-deep in his hair.

"I find it amazing," she whispered brokenly, "that you're looking for a marriage in name only."

He wasn't sure if she was being humorous or not, but he wasn't taking any chances. "We might need to revise that portion of the agreement."

"There won't be any agreement, Dash."

He was afraid of that. "Damn it, Savannah, would you kindly listen to reason? I wasn't looking to insult you . . . I thought you'd like the idea."

"Think again." She was working fast and feverishly at righting her clothes, but her fingers seemed uncooperative at best. Dash didn't volunteer to help, instinctively knowing she wouldn't welcome his efforts. He doubted that he would have done much good anyway. His control, now more so than earlier, was stretched to the breaking point. The hard truth was, Savannah hadn't a clue what she did to him, caught as she was, fighting the effect he had on her.

"Are you willing to listen to reason?" he asked, hoping he'd reached her, if on no level other than physical. After their brief interlude she should realize he was serious.

"I've had to deal with a certain amount of cruelty in my life," she whispered, her voice wobbling uncontrollably. "Children are often brutal with their taunts and their name-calling. It was something I became accustomed to as a child. It hurt. Sticks and stones may break your bones, but words cut far deeper. I would have rather taken a physical beating than listen to the names they called me."

"Savannah, for the love of heaven, stop." That she would compare his proposal to the ridicule she'd endured as a child was too painful to hear.

She stiffened, her back as straight as a nail. "I don't want to see you again."

The words hit him hard. "Why the hell not?"

She opened the car door and awkwardly stepped into the alley. Her leg seemed to be bothering her and with some effort she shifted her weight. "I don't trust myself with you . . . and I don't trust you with me, either. I've got to take care of myself."

"I want to help you, not hurt you," he insisted.

She hung her head and Dash suspected she did so to hide the fact she was crying. "You make me wish I were whole—and I never will be. Goodbye, Dash. Please don't try to see me again. . . . Don't make this any more difficult than it already is."

Two weeks later, Dash's sister, Susan, strolled into Savannah's shop. Savannah experienced a sense of warm appreciation and awe at the happiness that shone from the young woman's eyes.

"What are you doing here?" Savannah asked. "You're supposed to be on your honeymoon."

"We're been back for several days."

Following the wedding, Savannah rarely saw her clients. Whenever someone made the effort to stop in at the shop, it was a special treat. More so with Susan because Savannah had been actively involved in the wedding. Actively involved with Dash, if she were willing to be honest, which at the moment, she wasn't.

"You look—" Savannah searched for the right word "—beautiful." The two women hugged and Savannah squeezed her friend tightly as the unexpected tears moistened her eyes. She didn't allow them to fall, not wanting Susan to see how emotional she'd become. "I've missed you," she said, but more appropriately, she'd missed Dash.

"Dash said the same thing. You both knew before I was married that I was moving to California with

Kurt. Now you're acting like it's a big shock. By the way, Kurt sends his love."

Savannah eased from her friend's embrace. "What are you doing back in Seattle so soon? Kurt's with you, isn't he?"

"Why I'm here is a long story. As to your second question, Kurt couldn't come. With the wedding and the honeymoon, he couldn't get away. It's the first time we've been apart and I miss him dreadfully already." A wistful look came over her.

"What brings you to Seattle?"

Susan hesitated just a fraction of a second. "Dash."

So her big brother had sent her. This was exactly what she should have expected from Dash. The man wasn't fair—he'd use any means at his disposal to achieve his purpose.

"He doesn't know I'm here," Susan said as if reading Savannah's thoughts. "He'd be furious if he ever found out. I phoned him when Kurt and I arrived home from our honeymoon and he said he was having several pieces of furniture shipped to us. Items that had once belonged to our parents. I was a little surprised since we're living in a small apartment and don't have much space. Dash knows that. Kurt talked to him, too, and afterward we agreed something was wrong. The best way to handle the situation was for me to visit."

"I see." Savannah made busywork around her desk, straightening a stack of papers, rearranging pens in their holder. "How is Dash?"

"Miserable. I don't know why and he's doing an admirable job of pretending otherwise. He's spending a lot of time at the office. Apparently he's tied up with an important case."

"Divorce?" Savannah asked unnecessarily. That was his specialty—driving a wedge deeper and deeper between two people who'd once loved each other, enhancing misery and heartache. Each divorce he handled lent credence to his pessimistic views on marriage. That wasn't going to change, and she was living in a fool's world if she believed otherwise.

"You might have read about this case. It's been in all the papers. It's the one with Don Griffin, the man who owns all those great seafood restaurants. It's really sad."

Savannah did remember reading something about it. Apparently Mr. Griffin had become involved with much younger woman. It was a story as old as time and equally pathetic. She hadn't realized Dash was involved, but should have. He was Seattle's top divorce attorney, and naturally a man as wealthy and influential as Don Griffin would hire the very best.

"I know the case," Savannah admitted.

"Dash's been working late every night." She paused and waited for Savannah to comment.

"He enjoys his work."

"He used to, but I'm not so sure anymore. Something's really bothering him."

Their conversation was making Savannah uncomfortable. "I'm sorry to hear that."

"It's more than what's going on at the law firm, though. Kurt and I both think it has something to do with you, but when I asked him, Dash nearly bit my head off. He wouldn't even talk about you."

Savannah smiled softly to herself. "Neither will I. Sometimes it's better to leave well enough alone. We both appreciate your love and support, but what's going on between me and Dash is our own business. Leave it at that, please."

"All right." Susan wasn't happy about that, Savannah could tell, but the last thing Dash and she wanted or needed was Susan and Kurt meddling in their lives. Susan looked regretfully at the time. "I have to get back. The movers are coming this afternoon. I'm not taking much—we simply don't have the room for it. Several of the items belong to Dash, anyway. I don't know why he insisted on shipping us the rocking horse. Dad built it for him when he was just a baby and it was understood that Dash would hand it down to his own children. It's been in the basement for years. I don't know why he felt it was so necessary to send it to me, especially now. Kurt and I aren't planning to start a family for a couple of years. Men just don't make sense sometimes."

"You're only discovering that now?" Savannah teased.

Susan laughed. "I should know better after living all those years with my brother."

They hugged and Susan left shortly afterward.

The day was exceptionally slow, and with time on her hands, Savannah sat at her desk and drew a design for a flower arrangement. Intent on her task, she went on for several moments before she realized that it wasn't a flower arrangement that was taking shape on the sheet of white paper, but a child's rocking horse.

Savannah hesitated and set the pencil aside. The loneliness of her existence had rarely hit with greater impact. She covered her face with her hands. The rocking horse symbolized the child she would never have, the husband who would only be a figment of her dreams. It spelled out in bright, bold letters written with the pain of her isolation that she would be instrumental in bringing happiness to others, but would never find it herself.

"What do you mean Janice has turned down our settlement proposal?" Don Griffin shouted. He propelled his large frame from the chair across from Dash's desk and started pacing. His movements were abrupt and disjointed. "It was a fair offer, more than fair. You said so yourself."

"This is the way these matters work, Mr. Griffin. As I explained earlier, if you'll recall, it was a little unlikely that your wife and her attorney would accept our first offer. It's just the way the game is played. If you think of it as though you're negotiating for a new car, it might help. Your wife's attorney wouldn't be earning his fee if he didn't raise some objections."

"How much longer is this going to drag on?" his client demanded. "I want this over with quickly, do you understand? Give Janice what she wants. What the hell do I care, anyway? If she insists on taking control of the restaurants, fine, she can have them. She can have the house, the car, our investments, too, for all I care."

"I can't allow you to do that."

"Why the hell not?" He slammed his hand down against the desk top, the sound reverberating across the room like a sonic boom.

"You've hired me to represent you in a court of law, to take care of your interests. If you make a decision now based on emotion, you'll regret it later. These matters take time."

"I haven't got time," the tall, stocky man insisted. Don Griffin was in his early fifties, and beginning to show his age.

"Is there a reason we need to rush?" Dash hated surprises. If Don's girlfriend was pregnant, he didn't want to find out about it in the courtroom.

"Yes," the other man shouted. "There's a damn good reason. I hate this constant barrage of fighting, of having my reputation raked over the coals in the afternoon paper. Twenty-seven years of marriage and after one minor indiscretion, Janice makes me look like a serial murderer. Did you know the restaurant's receipts dropped ten percent after that story was leaked to the press?"

Dash didn't know who was responsible for that, but he could take an educated guess. Janice Griffin's attorney, Tony Pound, had a reputation for stirring up controversy whenever possible, especially if it helped his case.

Dash made a notation of the lost revenue and decided that when he phoned Tony later this afternoon, he'd let it be known Janice might not have nearly as big a compensation as she'd previously hoped.

"Don't let anyone tell you negative publicity doesn't hurt," Don continued. "If it continues like this much longer, we may be filing for bankruptcy next."

"I'll make sure Mr. Pound learns this."

"Good, and while you're at it," Don said, waving his finger at Dash, "do what you can about me seeing my daughter. Janice can't keep me away from Amy, and this bull about me being a negative influence on our daughter is exactly that—bull."

"I'll arrange visitation rights for you as soon as I can."

"See if I can have her this weekend. I'm going to the beach and Amy's always loved the beach. But don't tell Janice where I'm taking her. She's paranoid about Amy going anywhere close to the water."

"I'll see what I can do. Is there anything else?"

His client continued to pace, rubbing his hands together as if warding off a chill. "Have you seen my wife and daughter recently?" he asked, not looking at Dash.

"No. That would be highly unusual. Is there a reason why you're asking?"

"I . . . I was just wondering how they looked, is all. If they're well. It's no big deal."

It was there in the eyes, Dash noted, the way it always was. The pain, the loneliness, the sense of loss so strong, it brought powerful men and women to their knees. Dash thought of these moments when clients realized they were about to lose what they'd once considered life's most important anchor. Their chains were broken. Foundations they'd once considered solid proved not to be so invincible. With their anchors split, it became a struggle to keep from drifting. Storms quickly arrived and it was then that Dash learned the truth about his clients. Some weathered these tempests and came out on the other side stronger and more confident. Others struggled to stay afloat and eventually drowned in their foolishness.

Sadly, he didn't know on which side Don Griffin would fall.

The sense of urgency in her father's voice was what struck Savannah first. The phone call came in the middle of her busiest time of day. His words were a cloud and it took several moments for her to decipher what he was saying.

"Mom's in the hospital?" Savannah repeated. Her blood ran cold at the thought.

"Yes." Her father, who was always so calm and collected, was near panic. "She collapsed at home.... I didn't know what to do so I called an aid car and they've brought her to the hospital. The doctors are with her now."

"I'll be there in five minutes," Savannah promised.

She'd always hated the smell in a hospital, she realized as she rushed into the emergency entrance of Northend Memorial. The scent rushed at her like a powerful spray, resurrecting memories she'd pushed to the farthest reaches of her mind.

Savannah found her father sitting in the emergency room, his shoulders hunched over, his eyes round and empty. "Daddy," she whispered, "what happened?"

"I...don't know. We were working in the yard when your mother called out to me. By the time I turned around she'd passed out. I was afraid for a moment that she was dead. I nearly panicked."

Savannah sat in the seat next to him and reached for his hand. Their fingers intertwined.

"I forgot about you not liking hospitals," her father said apologetically.

"It's all right. I wouldn't want to be anyplace else but here with you."

"I'm scared, sweetheart, really scared."

"I know." Savannah was, too. "Have you talked to the doctors yet?"

Her father shook his head. "How long will it take? She's been in there over an hour."

"Anytime now, I'm sure." At the moment, Savannah wasn't sure of anything, least of all how her father would cope without her mother. It was unfair that this should happen now when they were in the prime of their lives. Unfair that their dreams had been cut short before they had a chance to live them out.

"Mr. Charles." The doctor approached them then, his face revealing his concern.

Savannah and her father stood, as if they wanted to be planted firmly on their feet, braced and ready for tragedy, when they heard the news.

"Your wife's suffered a stroke."

In the past few weeks, Dash had made it a habit to stay late at the office. It was an excuse and he knew it. He didn't like spending time at the house. It'd been nearly a month since Savannah had been inside his home and he swore each time he walked inside, he caught a whiff of her perfume. It drove him to distraction. He'd taken to placing air fresheners at strategic points in an effort to do away with her special scent.

Sleeping in his bed caused additional problems. Savannah had left her imprint there, as well. When he woke in the morning, he could sense her presence with him. He could almost hear her breathing, feel her breath moist against his neck, her mouth scant inches from his own. It bothered the hell out of him that a woman could have this powerful effect on him.

She'd meant what she said about severing the relationship. Not that he'd expected to hear from her again. He hoped he would, but that was entirely different from expecting her to call.

More times than his pride cared to count, he'd resisted the need to contact her. He'd considered sending flowers with a humorous note, something to break the ice, to salvage his pride and her own, then decided against it.

She'd made herself crystal clear and he had no option but to abide by her wishes. She didn't want to see him again. So she wouldn't. The next move, if there was one, was hers to make.

As for the ridiculous proposal of marriage... Seldom had he regretted anything more. It embarrassed him to think about it, so he avoided doing so whenever possible.

Someone knocked softly on his door. He checked his watch, surprised to discover he wasn't alone.

"Come in."

The door opened and Savannah stood on the other side. She was pale, her features ashen, her eyes red rimmed as if she'd recently been crying.

"Savannah," he said, coming around his desk. "What's wrong?" He resisted the urge to reach for her and hold her, not knowing if she'd welcome his touch and not wanting to chance it.

"I've come," she said in a voice that was devoid of emotion, "to tell you I've reconsidered. I'll accept your offer of a marriage of convenience.... That is, if it's still open."

Chapter Ten

"You're sure about this?" Generally Dash wasn't one to look a gift horse in the mouth, but this time was the exception. Something had happened to cause Savannah to change her mind, something drastic. Dash was convinced of that.

"I wouldn't be here if I wasn't sure this is what I want." Nervously she reached inside her purse and took out a well-creased slip of paper. "I've made up a list of matters we need to discuss first...if you're willing."

"All right." He gestured toward the chair and sat down himself. "But first tell me what's happened."

"My mother," she began, and paused as her lower lip began to tremble. It took a couple of moments before she was composed enough to continue speaking without revealing her emotions. "Mom's in the hospital.... She had a stroke. Her prognosis for a complete recovery is excellent, but it frightened me terribly...Dad, too.''

"I'm sorry to hear that.''

"Mom's stroke helped me realize that I might not have my parents much longer. I refuse to allow them to sacrifice their dreams because of me."

"I see."

She unfolded the piece of paper in her hands. "Are you ready to discuss the details?"

"By all means." He reached for his gold pen and a fresh legal pad.

"There will be no...lovemaking. You mentioned earlier that you preferred this to be a marriage of convenience, and I'm in full agreement."

That had been a hasty suggestion, certainly not one he'd carefully thought out. In light of their strong physical attraction for one another, Dash didn't believe this stipulation would hold up more than a few days, a week at the most. The minute he kissed her, or took her in his arms, the powerful, compelling chemistry they shared would return. Savannah might be able to deny the electricity, but it was a tad more difficult for a man.

"You're sure about this?" he asked.

"Positive."

Suggesting they wouldn't be able to keep their hands off each other was grounds for a heated argument in which Savannah was sure to accuse him of being arrogant and superior. Dash decided to agree with her for the present and let time prove him right.

"Do you agree?" Her eyes challenged him to defy her. Dash estimated it'd take a bulldozer to break through her defenses now.

He rolled the pen between his palms and relaxed in his leather chair, not wishing to give her a reason to suspect his reservations. ''If a marriage in name only is what you want, then naturally I'll agree to those terms.''

''Good.'' She nodded once, much too enthusiastically to suit him.

''Unless we mutually agree otherwise at some point,'' he added.

Savannah's eyes darted back to his. ''I wouldn't count on that if I were you. I'm agreeing to this marriage for one reason and one reason only. I want to be sure you understand that.''

''In other words, you don't plan to trick me into falling in love with you.'' He heard the edge in his own voice and regretted it. Savannah had sacrificed her pride the minute she'd walked through his door; goading wasn't necessary.

''This isn't a game to me, Dash. I'm serious. If you aren't, maybe we should call it quits right now.''

''I was the one who suggested this,'' he reminded her, not bothering to mention that it had been a spur-of-the-moment idea he'd regretted every second since. He stared at Savannah, noting the changes in her. Her voice was sharp and abrupt. He'd always viewed her as delicate and softly feminine. She was that and more. Much more. There was a sharpness to her now, a hard protective shell that she wore like a second skin. She didn't trust him not to hurt her. Didn't trust him not to destroy her once-unshakable faith in love and the institution of marriage.

''I'll draw up the papers to read that this will be a marriage of convenience unless we mutually agree otherwise. Does that satisfy you?''

"All right, as long we understand each other." Her gaze fell to her list and she moved her finger down a notch on the wrinkled sheet. "The second item I have written down has to do with our living arrangements. I'll agree to move in with you for only a brief period of time."

"How brief?" This didn't sound any more encouraging than the first stipulation.

"Until my mother's well enough to travel south. That is the reason I'm willing to go through with this, after all. But to be as fair as possible, I'll stay with you until a senior partner's named."

"I'd appreciate that." The announcement would come within the month, Dash was certain, although it was taking much longer than he'd anticipated. He'd like nothing better than to pull a fast one on Paul. The pompous ass would likely leave the firm. Dash smiled just thinking about it.

"After that there won't be any need for us to continue this farce. I'll move back to my home and we can have the marriage, such as it is, dissolved. Of course, I'll make no claims on you financially and I'd expect the same."

"Of course," Dash agreed. Yet this talk of divorce so soon after marriage grated against his pride. It wouldn't look good for him with John Stackhouse and Arnold Sterle if he were only to be married a few weeks. "For propriety's sake, I'd like to suggest we stay married a year."

"A year," she repeated, making it sound as if that were a lifetime.

It wouldn't be so bad, especially if she intended on moving out after a few weeks. They might even find it advantageous to continue with the charade for a number of years, depending on how they felt. Suggesting this now didn't seem appropriate. He'd play it safe and wait; when the time came they could reevaluate the situation.

"Anything else?" he asked, after making a second notation on the legal pad.

"Yes, as a matter of fact, I have several items listed."

Dash groaned inwardly, but presented a calm exterior.

"While I'm living with you, I insist we sleep in separate bedrooms. To my way of thinking, the less we have to do with one another, the better. You live your life the same as always and I'll live mine."

Dash wrote this down, as well, but made a point of hesitating, making sure she was aware of his uneasiness with this latest dictate. This would be the ideal setup if he were looking for a roommate, but Dash was seeking a deeper commitment.

"Since you mention propriety..." Savannah said and stiffened, her back as straight as a stickpin.

"Yes?" he prompted when she didn't immediately continue.

"Although our marriage will be one of convenience, I feel strongly that the two of us should practice a certain code of ethics." The words were rushed, as if she expected him to disagree. "I expect you to discontinue dating other women," she continued, slower now. "If I were to discover that you had been seeing someone else, I would consider that immediate grounds for divorce."

"The same would hold true for you," he returned calmly. It caused him to wonder what kind of man she thought him to be. "If I were to learn you were interested in another man, then I would see no reason to continue our agreement."

"That isn't likely to happen," she blurted out defensively.

"Any more than it is with me."

She clamped her mouth closed and Dash guessed she didn't believe him. He wondered where she'd gotten the impression he was a playboy. It was true that following his divorce he'd occasionally dated over the years, but there'd never been anyone he was serious about until he'd met Savannah. "We'll need to be convincing," she said next, her voice wavering slightly, "otherwise my parents, especially my father, will see through this ploy in an instant. They aren't likely to be easily fooled, and it's important we persuade them this is a love match."

"I can be convincing." He'd gained his reputation swaying a twelve-member jury; an elderly couple who wanted to believe he was in love with their daughter would be a piece of cake by comparison.

"I'll do my best to be the same," Savannah assured him, relaxing slightly. She neatly folded the sheet of paper, running her fingers along the crease line. "Was there anything you wanted to add?"

Without time to think over their agreement, Dash was at a disadvantage. "I might later."

"I…was hoping we could come to terms as quickly as possible so I can tell my parents right away."

"We'll tell them together," Dash said. "Otherwise they'll find it odd. What do you want to do about the actual wedding ceremony?"

She looked away, then lowered her gaze. "I wasn't sure you'd agree so I hadn't given it much thought. I guess I should have seen that, arranging weddings for a living."

"Don't look so chagrined. This isn't anything like a normal, run-of-the-mill marriage."

"Exactly," she was quick to concur. "I'd like a small gathering. My parents and a few good friends—no more than ten or so. What about you?"

"About that number." He'd make sure Sterle and Stackhouse received invitations.

"I'll arrange for the ceremony, then, followed by dinner. Is that agreeable?"

He shrugged, not really caring. The actual wedding was a necessary evil. Small and private appealed to him far more than the lavish gathering Susan had had. At least Savannah wasn't going to subject him to that, although he felt mildly guilty to be cheating her out of a fancy wedding.

"How long do you think you'll need to come up with any further stipulations?" she asked.

"Not long," he promised, but one matter slipped into his mind and he mentioned it before censuring the thought. "I'd like it if we made a habit of eating dinner together."

"Dinner?" Savannah repeated, sounding incredulous.

In light of her reaction, his one condition of marriage did sound a tad bizarre. If they were going through the trouble of getting married, it seemed a shame that they work so hard at remaining strangers. "We need to make a point of spending some time together, don't you think?"

"I don't see where that'll be necessary."

"It will be if we're going to give the facade of being married. We'll need to be in tune with what's going on in each other's lives."

Her agreeing nod was reluctant. "I see your point."

"We can share the housework, so you don't need to worry about me sticking you with the cooking and the cleanup afterward. I want to be fair about this."

"That sounds equitable."

"I don't intend to take advantage of you, Savannah." It was important she believe that, although it was obvious she didn't. When they'd first discussed his proposal, she'd assumed Dash was using her handicap to his advantage. She was wrong then and more so now. Even married to Savannah, he didn't hold out much hope of becoming a senior partner. Not when Paul Justice was ingratiating himself to anyone and everyone who could advance his career. But if there was even the slightest possibility he might beat out Paul, Dash was willing to risk it. His dislike for the man increased daily, especially since Paul had made such a fuss. He deeply resented that Dash had been given the Don Griffin case over him.

"What day should I arrange the wedding for?" Savannah asked, flipping through the pages of a small pocket calendar.

"In a week, if at all possible." He could tell by the way her eyes widened that she expected to be given more time. "Is that too soon?"

"Not really.... A week shouldn't be much of a problem, although it'll raise a few questions."

"How's that?"

"People are going to ask questions, don't you think?"

"So? Does that bother you?"

"Not exactly."

"Good." Dash had little success in hiding a smile.

"In that case, I think it'd be a good idea if you wrote up an agreement right away," she said. "You can add whatever provisions you want and if I disagree, I'll cross them off."

"That sounds fair enough. When would you like to tell your parents?"

"As soon as possible."

Dash stood and replaced his gold pen in the marble holder. "Then let's do that first thing. Is your mother still in the hospital?"

Savannah nodded. "Dad spends almost every minute of every day with her. The nurses told me they tried to send him home that first night, but he refused and ended up sleeping on the empty bed next to her."

"He's taken this hard, hasn't he?"

Savannah nodded. "He's worried sick.... That's the main reason I decided to accept your proposal. Mom loves the sunshine and I can't think of any place she'd enjoy recuperating more than in Arizona with her friends."

"In that case, we'll do what we can to be sure that happens."

"Oh, Savannah." Her mother's eyes glistened with the sheen of unshed tears as she sat up in her hospital bed. "You're going to be married."

Dash slipped his arm around Savannah's waist with familiar ease and smiled down on her as if the sun rose and set in her eyes. "I know my timing couldn't be worse," Dash admitted, "but I hope you'll find it in your heart to forgive me."

"There's nothing to forgive. We're thrilled, aren't we, Marcus?" Her mother smiled blissfully. Dash was eating up the attention, nuzzling Savannah's neck, planting moist kisses when he was sure her parents would notice. These open displays of affection were unlike him and were fast beginning to irritate Savannah.

"This does seem rather sudden, though, doesn't it?" her father asked nonchalantly.

Savannah knew convincing her father would be much more difficult than persuading her mother. Dash must have realized it, too, because he was playing the role as if he expected to earn an award for his performance as the besotted lover.

"Savannah and I've been dating off and on all summer. Isn't that right, darling?" He brought her close to his side and dropped a quick kiss on the side of her neck. The moment they were alone, she'd kindly thank him to keep his casual kisses to himself. Every time he bounced his lips over her skin, a shiver of awareness raced up her spine. Dash knew it; otherwise he wouldn't take every opportunity to make her so uncomfortable.

"Are you in love?" her father asked her directly.

"Marcus, what a thing to ask," her mother said with an embarrassed laugh. "Savannah and Dash have come to us wanting to share wonderful news. This isn't any time to ask a lot of silly questions."

"Would I marry Dash if I didn't love him?" Savannah asked, hoping that would be enough to reassure her parent. She was leaving the question open-ended, but she wasn't entirely sure he wouldn't read through that.

"We'd like to have the wedding as soon as possible," Dash added, looking down on her adoringly as if he couldn't bear to take his eyes off her.

"There's a rush?" Mr. Charles asked.

Her father's attitude surprised Savannah. She was prepared for a bit of skepticism, but not this interrogation. Once he was convinced Savannah loved Dash, she didn't figure there would be any problems.

"I want Savannah with me," Dash answered, "every minute of every day. It took me a long time to decide to marry again and now that I have, each day I have to wait to make her a part of my life feels like an eternity." He reached for her hand and raised it to his lips, where he planted a series of soft kisses on her knuckles. He was overdoing it, making a fool of them both, and Savannah fumed.

"You feel the same way about Dash?"

"Yes, Daddy," she returned smoothly.

"I've waited all my life for a woman like Savannah."

Savannah couldn't help it; she stepped on Dash's foot and he yelped, then glared at her accusingly.

"I'm sorry, darling, did I hurt you?" she asked sweetly.

"No, I'm fine." His eyes questioned her, but she ignored the silent entreaty.

Her father stood at the head of the bed, which was angled up so that her mother was in a sitting position. The couple was holding hands.

"Do you object to Savannah marrying Dash?" her father questioned.

Her mother's sigh was filled with relief and joy. "Savannah's far too old to require our approval, and you know it. She can do as she pleases. That Dash has come to ask for her hand in marriage is a sweet gesture. I don't understand why you're behaving like this is some tragedy when it's apparent our little girl is so happy. Isn't this what we've prayed for all these years?"

"I know it's come at you out of the blue, Daddy," Savannah whispered, the words sticking in her throat, "but you know me well enough to know I'd never marry a man I didn't love with my whole heart."

"The sooner Savannah's in my life, the sooner I can be complete," Dash added with a dramatic sigh.

Although he was clearly making an effort to sound sincere, it was all Savannah could do not to shove her finger down her throat. Anyone who knew Dash for any length of time would recognize he was lying, and doing a poor job of it. He made loving Savannah comparable to falling into a jar of honey, equating it with something sickeningly sweet. Anyone with a lick of sense would see through their charade in an instant. Her father was an intelligent man and wouldn't be easily fooled.

"I should be out of the hospital by Friday," her mother said excitedly. "That'll give me a couple of days to rest up at home before the wedding."

"If you need a few extra days to rest, we don't mind waiting. It's important that you be there, isn't that right, darling?"

Savannah felt the sharp end of his elbow against her ribs and quickly nodded. "Of course. Having you both there is more important than anything."

"You're sure?" her mother questioned.

"Absolutely positive."

Her father didn't seem nearly as convinced. "I don't understand why you insist upon holding the wedding so soon. You two barely know one another."

"We know each other better than you think," Dash said with the same familiarity with which he fondled her, kissing her at will. The insinuation that they were lovers was clear. It was all Savannah could manage not to claim otherwise. If Dash was looking for means of embarrassing her, he'd surpassed his wildest expectations. Her face felt fire engine red and her gaze refused to meet either of her parents'.

"I don't think we need to question Savannah and Dash any longer," her mother said, although it had taken her a couple of moments to recover. "They know their own minds. You have my blessing."

"Daddy?" Savannah whispered, holding her breath.

He didn't say anything, then nodded.

"There are a thousand things to attend to before Wednesday," Savannah said abruptly, bending over to kiss her mother's pale cheek. "If you don't mind, Dash and I'll leave now."

"Of course," her father said.

"Thank you so much for the wonderful news, sweetheart." Her mother was tiring, Savannah noted. Their leaving came at the opportune moment.

Savannah couldn't wait until they were well outside the hospital room before turning on Dash. "How dare you," she flared, her hands knotted into fists at her sides. The man infuriated her. He had no sense of decency, no sense of ethics. She'd felt it was important to be convincing, but Dash cheerfully went about making fools of them both. It angered her so much it was all she could do not to cry out for him to stop.

"What did I do?" he demanded, wearing that confused, injured look that was meant to promote sympathy. It wouldn't work—not this time, Savannah decided.

"You implied...you let my parents believe we were lovers," she told him, and that was just for starters.

"So?" Dash asked, apparently stumbling in the dark. "Good grief, Savannah, you're twenty-eight years old. They know you're not a virgin."

She punched the elevator button with enough force to injure her finger. The rush of tears was a mingling of outrage and indignation. She blinked furiously in an effort to keep them from spilling.

Dash exhaled softly and rubbed a hand over the back of his neck. "You're a virgin, aren't you?"

"Do you mind if we don't discuss such private matters in a public place?" she ground out between clenched teeth. The elevator arrived just then with a rushing sound and Savannah eagerly stepped on.

There were a couple of other people there who stared at her curiously. Her twisted leg often made her the center of attention, but she strongly suspected it was the tears that shone in her eyes that prompted the sympathetic looks.

She managed to hold her peace until they reached the parking lot. "As for that stupid declaration of being so crazy about me you couldn't wait another minute to make me yours, I had to stop myself from throwing up."

"What's wrong with that? You should be praising me instead of getting all bent out of shape."

"Praising you? For what?"

"Convincing your father we're in love."

"Oh, please," Savannah whispered, gazing toward the night sky. The heavens were clear as glass, the stars a handful of diamonds splashed across a bed of black velvet. It was all so beautiful, when she felt so terribly ugly. Dash was saying the things every woman longs to hear—beautiful words. Only, his were empty. Perhaps that was what troubled her so much, the fact that he didn't mean what he was saying when she wanted it all to be true.

"You're not making a damn bit of sense." His patience was gone as he unlocked the passenger door and then slammed it closed. The sharp sound shot out like a bullet. "Let's have this out right here and now."

"Fine," she challenged, more than willing to clear the air.

"I was doing everything I could think to convince your parents we're madly in love. Correct me if I'm wrong, but isn't that the objective?"

"You didn't need to lay it on so thick, did you?"

"What do you mean?"

"Did you have to hold on to me like you couldn't bear to be separated from me for a single second? The kissing has got to stop. I won't have you fawning all over me like a lovesick calf."

"Fine, I won't lay another hand on you as long as we're together. Not unless you ask."

"You make that sound like a distinct possibility."

He laughed shrewdly, but didn't reply. The look he gave her just then spoke volumes. Savannah found herself getting even angrier at him.

"You could practice being a bit more subtle, couldn't you?" she continued. "If anyone should know the power of subtlety, it should be you. I thought you were this top-notch attorney. Don't you know anything about human nature?''

"I know a little." He went strangely quiet for a moment. "You don't think we fooled your father?"

"No, Dash, I don't," she said, calmer now. "The only people we seem capable of duping is ourselves. I'm afraid this simply isn't going to work."

"You want out already?" he demanded, sounding shocked and surprised. "Our engagement isn't even three hours old and already you're breaking it."

"We don't have any choice," she insisted. "Anyone with a lick of sense is going to see through this charade in a heartbeat. If we can't handle announcing the news to my parents, how do you expect to get through the wedding ceremony?"

"We'll manage."

"How can you be so sure of that?" she pressed, not the least bit confident.

"We did before, didn't we?" he asked softly. "At Susan's wedding."

He would bring that up. The man didn't fight fair. The wedding ceremony had been her one slip of judgment and now he was waving it in front of her like a red flag, challenging her to a repeat performance. "But that wasn't real . . . we weren't the center of attention."

"We'll manage very well—just you wait and see."

Dash walked around to the front of his car and leaned against the hood, crossing his arms. "I suggest we continue as planned, wait until we hear from your family and then decide. Are you game?"

Personally, Savannah felt it was a waste of time, but for no reason she could decipher, she nodded. "All right. After what happened just now, I don't hold much faith in us getting past first base."

"Oh, ye of little faith," Dash said, walking around to her side of the car and holding the door open for her. "We've only just begun, and the very best is yet to come."

Savannah wished she could believe him.

Dash was busy at his desk, reviewing the latest settlement offer from Don Griffin, when his secretary buzzed him and announced Marcus Charles was there to see him without an appointment.

"Send him in," Dash instructed as his mind zoomed at laser speed. He closed the file, set it aside and stood.

Savannah's parent was a gentle man who reminded him a little of his own father. "Come in, please," Dash said pleasantly. "This is a surprise."

"I should have phoned."

"We all behave impulsively at one time or another," Dash said, hoping Savannah's father would catch the meaning. He'd tried hard to make it sound like their wedding plans were impulsive. He'd strived to convince her family he was crazy in love with her and, according to Savannah, he'd overplayed his hand. Perhaps she was right.

"Do you mind if I sit down?"

"Of course not," Dash said quickly, surprised by his lack of good manners. Apparently he was more shaken by this unforeseen visit than he realized. "Is there anything I can get you? Coffee, tea, a cold drink?"

"No, thanks." He claimed the chair across from Dash's and crossed his legs. "It looks like Joyce will be released from the hospital a day early."

Dash was relieved. "That's wonderful news."

"Yours and Savannah news rivaled that. The doctor seems to think it's what helped Joyce to recover so quickly."

"I'm pleased to hear that."

"It's going to take several months before she's fully recovered, but that's to be expected."

Dash nodded, not thinking any comment was necessary. He was rarely nervous, but he found himself that way now.

Marcus was silent for a moment. "You want to marry Savannah?"

"Yes, sir." This much was true and his sincerity must have rung clear in his response because it seemed to him that Savannah's father relaxed.

"My daughter has special needs."

"I'm well aware of her limitations, if that's what you're referring to," Dash said, not allowing the older man to elaborate.

"This doesn't bother you?"

"No," he answered honestly. "Should it?"

"No." Marcus stood then abruptly and walked over to the window. "I'm not going to ask if you love Savannah," he said abruptly. "For a number of reasons that doesn't matter to me as much as it did earlier. If you don't love her, you will soon enough. She's an incredible woman.

"You came to me the other night seeking my blessing and I'm giving it to you." He turned and held out his hand.

The two men exchanged hearty handshakes. When they'd finished, Marcus Charles reached inside his suit jacket, withdrew a business-size envelope and set it on Dash's desk.

"What's that?"

Marcus smiled. "Savannah's mother and I thought long and hard about what we should give you as a wedding present, then decided we would give you time alone together. Inside is a map to a remote cabin in the San Juan Islands. We're giving you one week of uninterrupted peace."

Chapter Eleven

"What did you expect me to do?" Dash demanded as they drove off the Washington State ferry. "Refuse your parent's wedding gift?" This marriage was definitely getting off to a rocky start. They'd been man and wife less than twelve hours and already they were squabbling.

"A remote cabin...alone together. I've never heard of anything more ridiculous."

"Most newlyweds would be thrilled with the idea."

"We're not like other couples."

"I don't need you to remind me of that," Dash snapped. "You try to do someone a favor..."

"Are you insinuating marrying me was a kindness?" Savannah was huddled so close to the door that she was in danger of falling out of the car on a sharp corner.

Dash prayed for patience. So this was what their marriage was going to be like—this constant barrage of insults, nit-picking at each other, faultfinding.

"No, Savannah, I don't consider marrying you a kindness. You're my wife and—"

"In name only," she threw out at him in icy tones.

"Does that mean we're enemies now?"

"Of course not."

"Then why is it we've been at each other's throat from the moment we left the wedding dinner? I'm sorry your family insisted we take a honeymoon. Trust me, I'm well aware you'd rather spend time with anyone else but me, but I was hoping we'd make the best of this."

She didn't answer him, which was just as well. The silence was a welcome contrast to the constant bickering that had been going on from the moment they were alone.

"It was a beautiful wedding," she said softly, unexpectedly.

"Yes, it was." Savannah was beautiful in her ivory silk suit with a short chiffon veil decorated with string pearls. Dash had barely been able to take his eyes off her. It was a struggle to remember this was a pretend marriage.

"I've been defensive," she added apologetically. "I'm sorry, Dash, for everything. It isn't your fault we're stuck together like this."

"It doesn't have to be a tragedy."

"You're right," she said, but she didn't sound as if she was convinced of the fact. "We might find we enjoy each other's company."

Dash stiffened, offended by the comment. He'd enjoyed being with Savannah from the beginning, enjoyed goading her, challenging her views on marriage. He'd found himself seeking her out, looking for excuses to be with her, until she'd insisted she didn't want to see him again. He'd abided by her wishes, but he'd missed her, far more than he cared to admit.

"I saw Mr. Sterle and Mr. Stackhouse talking to you after the ceremony."

Dash grinned and a sense of smug satisfaction settled over him. Both of the senior partners had been delighted to have Dash marry Savannah. She'd managed to completely captivate those two and had the pair in the palm of her hand. Arnold Sterle had been acutely disappointed that they'd decided against a wedding dance. He'd been counting on another spin around the floor with Savannah.

"Did they say anything about the decision for the senior partnership?" Savannah asked.

It irked him that she was already eager to get out of their arrangement. "No, but then, a wedding isn't exactly the place to be discussing business." He didn't mention that it was at his sister's reception that John Stackhouse had originally introduced the subject.

"I see." She sounded disappointed, and Dash's hands tightened around the steering wheel. Luckily the drive was a beautiful one through lush green Lopez Island. Although Dash had lived in Washington all his life, he'd never ventured into the San Juan Islands. When they drove off the ferry he was surprised by the quiet coves and breathtaking coastline. In an effort to fill their time, he'd arranged for him and Savannah to take a cruise and explore the northernmost boundary islands of Susia and Patos, which were the closest islands to the Canadian border. He'd wanted their honeymoon to be a memorable experience and planned a shopping excursion to Friday Harbor for another day. He'd read about the quaint shops, excellent restaurants and a whale museum. Women liked those sorts of things. It seemed now that his efforts were for naught. Savannah had no intention of enjoying these days together; she was determined to make the worst of this.

"Have your parents said anything about traveling south?"

"Not yet," she said, sounding disheartened.

"They might not, you know." In other words, she could be stuck living with him for the next several years, like it or not. The thought didn't appeal to him any more than it did her, he was sure. Especially if she continued with this attitude.

"How much farther is it to the cabin?" she asked stiffly. Dash wasn't exactly sure. He had a detailed map and instructions, but since he'd never been on Lopez Island, he wasn't any expert. "Soon, I suspect."

"Good."

"You're tired?"

"A little."

It'd been a full day. First the wedding, then the dinner followed by the drive to the ferry and the ride across Puget Sound. It would be dark within the hour and Dash had hoped they'd have reached the cabin before then.

He reached the turnoff in the road and followed a winding, narrow highway for several miles. Savannah was suspiciously silent, clenching her wedding bouquet in her hands as if it were a swift sword. He was mildly surprised she'd chosen to bring it with her.

He found the dirt road he was looking for that led to the cabin and slowly drove down it, grateful he had rented a four-wheel-drive vehicle. The route was filled with ruts, which didn't lend him a lot of confidence about this remote cabin. If this was any indication of what the house would be like, they'd be lucky to have electricity and running water.

He was wrong and knew it the minute he drove into the clearing. This was no cabin, but a luxurious house, built with a Victorian flair with a turret and wrap-around porch.

"Oh, my... it's lovely," Savannah whispered.

The house was a sight to behold all on its own, but the view of the water was majestic. The structure sat on its own peninsula, overlooking a panorama that was nothing short of breathtaking.

"I'll get the luggage," Dash said, hopping out of his bright red jeep. He thought better of it, hurried around to Savannah's side and helped her down.

With his hands around her waist, he lifted her onto the ground. He longed to hold her against him, to swing her into his arms and carry her over the threshold like any husband, but he knew he dare not. Savannah wouldn't welcome his touch and she'd assume he was making a mockery of this traditional wedding custom. That was the way she seemed to be dealing with things lately, distrusting him and his motives. She made marriage feel like an insult. If this attitude lasted much longer, they'd have the shortest marriage on record.

"I'll get the luggage," he said again, unnecessarily. At least if his hands were full, he wouldn't be tempted to reach for Savannah.

"I'll open the door," she suggested, and for the first time she sounded enthusiastic. She hurried ahead of him and he noticed how she favored her injured leg more so than usual. Sitting for any length of time must make movement more difficult for her. She rarely spoke of her leg, preferring to keep it a deep, dark secret. He wished he knew how to broach the subject, but every attempt had been met with bristly pride, as if she believed she'd be less of a person for sharing this imperfect part of herself.

She had the door opened when he joined her. Stepping inside the house was like moving back into the nineteenth century. The warmth of the past stepped forward to greet them with welcoming arms.

The living room was decorated with a mix of antiques and huge windows that created a room that seemed to glow in the setting sun.

"Oh, Dash," Savannah whispered, "I don't know when I've seen anything more beautiful."

"Me, neither," he said.

"Dad must have seen an advertisement for this house. He knows how much I love anything Victorian, especially houses."

Dash stashed that away in his storehouse of information about Savannah. When it came time to celebrate her birthday or Christmas he'd know what to buy her.

"I'll put these in the bedrooms," Dash said. He didn't like the idea of them sleeping separately, but he didn't have any choice. He'd agreed to do so until she changed her mind, and from the looks of things that could be well into the next century.

The master bedroom was equally attractive, with a huge four-poster mahogany bed. French lace curtains hung from the windows and the walls were papered in a cheery yellow design. He set down Savannah's suitcase and headed for the second bedroom, which was to be his own. It was originally intended to be a children's room, he realized. Instead of a wife to keep him warm at night, he was destined to stare at a wall with rows of tin soldiers smiling back at him. So much for romance!

Savannah woke early the following morning, the sunlight spilling in from the window filtering through the lace curtain until a spidery pattern reflected against the floor like a soft pillow. She yawned and saf up in bed. Surprisingly, she'd fallen asleep right away without the pathos she'd expected.

"You're a married woman," she said aloud, thinking she might believe it if she heard herself say it. Her wedding and all that led up to it remained unreal in her mind. Afterward she'd been a witch to Dash.

It took her a long time to understand why she'd behaved in such an uncharacteristic manner. It dawned on her just before she went to bed. She was lashing out at him, blaming him for making a farce of what she considered holy. Only, he wasn't to blame; they were in this marriage together. A union was advantageous to them both.

She heard him rummaging around the kitchen. The aroma of coffee flirted with her, urging her out of bed. She reached for her robe and stuffed her feet into slippers.

"'Morning," she said when she joined him. It looked as if he'd been up for hours. A jacket hung on a peg by the back door with a pair of rubber boots on the mat. His hair was wet, and he cupped a mug of steaming coffee and leaned against the kitchen counter.

"'Morning," he said, grinning broadly.

"You've been exploring." It hurt a little that he'd gone out without her, but she couldn't blame him. She hadn't been decent company of late. It wouldn't be much fun walking along the beach with her, since her gait was slow and awkward. She didn't blame him for going without her, but it still hurt.

"I took a walk along the beach. I found you something." He reached behind him and presented her with a perfectly formed sand dollar.

Savannah's hand closed around her prize.

"I wasn't sure, but I thought I might have seen a pod of whales. It's a little difficult to tell from this distance."

Savannah made busywork about the kitchen, pouring herself a cup of coffee and checking the refrigerator for milk, all the while struggling to hold back her disappointment. She would have loved to have seen a pod of whales, even from a distance.

"What would you like for breakfast?" she asked, hoping to get their day off to a better start.

"Bacon, eggs, toast and a kiss."

Savannah froze.

"You heard me right. Come on, Savannah, loosen up a little. We're supposed to be madly in love, remember? This isn't going to work if you continue to act the part of the outraged virgin."

What he said was true, but that didn't make it any easier to swallow. In fact, his words stuck in her throat. She turned away from him and battled down an odd, confused mixture of anger and pain. She wanted to blame him, and knew she couldn't. She longed to stamp her foot, as she had when she was a child, and cry out, "No more." No more discord. No more silliness. But it wouldn't do any good. She was married, but destined to a life of loneliness. These were supposed to be the happiest days of her life and here she was struggling not to weep.

Dash had moved behind her and placed his hands against her shoulders. "Do you find me so repugnant?" he whispered close to her ear.

His warm breath was moist and so close, she shut her eyes and shook her head.

"Then why won't you let me kiss you?"

She shrugged her shoulders, but she was profoundly aware of the answer. If Dash kissed her, she'd remember how much she enjoyed his touch. It'd been like that from the beginning. He knew it. She knew it. Now he intended to use the information against her.

He brought his mouth down to her neck and rubbed his face back and forth against the gentle slope of her neckline. Shivers of awareness scooted up and down her spine, chilling her. Needing something to hold on to, Savannah reached for the kitchen counter.

"One kiss," he coaxed. "Just one."

"Y-you promise?"

"Of course. Anything you say."

She made a small, involuntary movement to turn around. His hands on her shoulders aided the process. She quivered when his mouth met hers and a familiar heat began to warm her insides. As always, their need for each other was so hot and intense, it frightened her. She parted her lips to his and a host of sensations assailed her as his tongue probed hers. Her breasts were pressed against the strong, muscular planes of his chest and her nipples tingled and ached with need.

Slowly, with reluctance and regret, he lifted his mouth from hers. "Do you want me to stop?" he asked in a husky whisper.

Savannah made an unintelligible sound.

"That's what I thought," he said eagerly, claiming her mouth again. Her lips parted, instantly impatient to accept his tongue and experience the mingling of pleasure and hungry demand being in his arms ultimately produced. This was what she was afraid would happen. This was what she wanted to happen.

Moments earlier, when his mouth had nuzzled her neck, she'd experienced shivers. She wasn't cold now, but hot—so hot she felt as if she were burning up inside.

Needing to ground herself, she locked her arms around his neck. Soon the kissing wasn't enough and she was wriggling against him, rubbing her body against his. She felt the hardness of his sex bulging against her. His power excited her and she softly sighed.

"Yes, baby," he whispered frantically. "That's it, that's it." His hands cupped her buttocks, half lifting her from the kitchen floor. He was working up the fabric of her nightgown and swore when he realized she didn't have anything on underneath.

Savannah felt as though her body were on fire. She'd been empty and lonely for so long. No man had ever kissed her like this. No man had ever wanted her so badly.

His hands were moving against her bottom, his stance wide to allow her body to nestle against his. Every movement of her hips seemed to add to the excitement, his and hers. She was soft and needy, he was hard and giving.

"You don't want me to stop, do you?" he begged. "Don't tell me you want me to stop."

Incapable of making a decision, she made a second unintelligible sound.

"If we continue like this, we're going to end up making love on the kitchen floor," Dash whispered.

"I don't know what I want," she whimpered.

"Yes, you do. Savannah, for the love of heaven, if it gets much hotter, we're both going to explode. Let me make love to you."

She started to protest, but he stopped her, dragging his mouth back to hers. He was perfect and she was impaired. He was strong and she was fragile. He needed her. Only she could satisfy him, his kisses seemed to be saying. Savannah didn't know if he was telling her this or if she was hearing it in her mind. It didn't matter; she got his message.

"No," she said with a whimper. She couldn't give him her body. If they made love, he'd own her completely, and she couldn't allow that to happen. Someday he was going to turn and walk away from her. Someday he was going to announce that it had all been great fun, but it was over and she was supposed to go her merry way without him. She was supposed to pretend it didn't matter.

"You don't mean that," Dash pleaded. "You can't tell me you don't want me." The words were issued in a heated whisper. "Damn it, Savannah, don't do this."

She buried her face in his shoulder. "Please...don't. You promised. You said you'd stop...whenever I asked."

He released her then, slowly, her body dragging against his as her feet slid back to the floor. She stepped away from him, anxious to break the contact, desperately needing room to breathe. She pressed her hand to the neckline of her gown and drew deep breaths of oxygen into her lungs.

Dash's eyes were squeezed shut and his teeth were locked as he struggled to bring himself back under control. When he opened them, Savannah swore they were filled with fire.

Without a word to her, he reached for his jacket, opened the door and walked out.

Savannah was trembling so hard, she had to pull out a chair and sit down. She didn't know how long she was there before she felt strong enough to stand, walk back into the bedroom and dress.

It was a mistake to allow him to kiss her; she'd known it even as she agreed, known it would be like this between them. Gnawing on her lower lip, she argued with herself, damning Dash and herself. They'd created an impossible situation, drawn up a list of rules and regulations and then insisted upon testing each one to the limits of their endurance. This was destined to be an interesting year.

She'd just finished placing their coffee cups in the dishwasher when the back door opened and Dash appeared. She paused and studied him. He looked calm and serene outwardly, but she wasn't fooled. She read the angry glint in his eyes loud and clear.

"If you're looking for an apology, you can forget it," he said.

"I ... don't blame you."

"Good, because you asked for that, whether you're willing to admit it or not."

"I understand." Now didn't seem the time to mention that he hadn't helped matters any by suggesting the kiss. Neither of them required a crystal ball to know what would happen when they started flirting with the physical aspect of their relationship. They were experimenting with fire.

Dash poured himself a cup of coffee. "Let's sit down and talk this out."

"I . . . don't know what there is to say," she said, preferring to avoid the issue completely. "It was a very human thing to happen. You're an attractive, healthy man with . . . needs."

"And you're a red-blooded woman. You have *needs,* too."

"I'd prefer to forget that."

"I'm sure you would. It takes more honesty than you're willing to admit, doesn't it?"

Savannah found the remark insulting, but then, Dash didn't seem inclined to be generous with her. Since she didn't have an argument to give him, she let it pass.

"I did some thinking while I walked off my frustration."

"Oh?" She was curious what he'd decided, but didn't want to press him.

"The way I see it, I'm setting myself up for significant levels of frustration if we have any more bouts like this last one. If you want to come out of this marriage as pristine as the freshly fallen snow, then far be it for me to butt my head against a brick wall."

"I'm not sure I understand."

"You don't need to. You have your wish, Savannah. I won't touch you again, not until you ask me, and the way I feel right now, you're going to have to do a whole lot more than ask. You're going to have to beg.''

Dash hadn't known it was possible for two human beings to live the way he and Savannah had spent the past two weeks. The so-called honeymoon had been bad enough, but back in civilization, living in this house, the situation had gone from unbearable to even worse. The electricity between them had enough amperage to light up a small city. He couldn't come close to her without feeling the static pull of her body. Yet they continued to ignore their mutual attraction.

They lived as brother and sister. They slept in separate rooms, politely inquired about each other's day, sat across the table from each other each night and made courteous conversation.

In two weeks Dash hadn't so much as held her hand. He dared not for fear he'd get burned. Not with her rejection, but with their need for each other.

Part of the problem was the fact that Savannah was a virgin. She didn't know what she was missing, but she had a fairly good idea, and that added a substantial element of intrigue. He sincerely hoped she was miserable, at least as miserable as he was.

''Mr. Griffin is here to see you,'' his secretary announced.

Dash stood to greet his client. Don Griffin had lost a considerable amount of weight in the past month. Dash had, too, come to think of it. He didn't have much of an appetite and was working out at the gym most nights. No one ever told him marriage was a great way of building muscle. Then again, no one had bothered to tell him what all this frustration would do to a man's nerves.

"Did you hear from Janice's attorney?" Don demanded first thing.

"Not yet."

"Does he normally take this long to return phone calls?" Agitated, Don started to pace the office. His client was looking a little under the weather, too, Dash noted.

"He does when he wants us to sweat," he explained.

"I want you to raise Janice's monthly allotment by five hundred dollars."

Dash sighed inwardly. This was proving to be a difficult case and not for the usual reasons. "Sit down, Mr. Griffin," Dash instructed. "Please," he added.

Don complied and sat down. He bounced his fingers against each other and studied Dash as he leaned back in his chair.

"Janice hasn't requested any extra money," Dash said.

"She might need it. Amy, too. There are a hundred unexpected expenses that crop up. I don't want her scrimping along. It's important to me that my wife and daughter live comfortably."

"You've been more than generous already."

"Just do as I say. I'm not paying you to argue with me."

"No, you're paying me for advice and I'm about to give you some, so kindly listen. This doesn't come cheap."

Don snorted loudly. "Tell me about it. I just got your last bill."

Dash smiled. It shocked his clients when they learned how expensive a divorce could be. Not only monetarily, but emotionally and physically. Dash had seen it happen more times than he cared to think about. Once his clients realized how costly a divorce could be, they were too embroiled in bitterness and it was impossible to undo the damage.

"Do you know what you're doing, giving Janice extra money?" Dash asked.

"Sure I do. I'm attempting to take financial care of my wife and daughter."

"You're already adequately doing so. Offering them more money is one way you have of easing your conscience. You're looking to absolve your guilt because you had an affair."

"It wasn't an affair," Don shouted. "It was a one-night thing, a momentary lapse that I've regretted every moment since. Janice would never have found out about it if it hadn't been for—never mind, that doesn't matter now. She found out about it and immediately contacted an attorney."

"My point is, she learned of your indiscretion and now you're looking to buy your peace of mind. Unfortunately, it doesn't work like that."

"All I'm looking to do is get this divorce over with."

Tony Pound, Janice's attorney, wasn't a fool. He knew exactly what he was doing, dragging these proceedings out as long as possible to prolong the guilt and the agony. To Dash's way of thinking, his client had been punished enough.

"This is one mistake you aren't going to be stuck paying monetarily for for the rest of your life," Dash assured him. "That's why John Stackhouse asked that I take your case. You've paid enough. You've lost your wife, your home, your daughter. That's more than enough. Now go back to your apartment, relax, and I'll contact you when I hear from Mr. Pound."

Don Griffin nodded reluctantly. "I don't know how much more of this I can take."

"It shouldn't be much longer," Dash assured him.

He rose slowly, awkwardly from the chair. "You'll be in touch soon?"

Dash nodded. Don Griffin left the office and Dash sat down to review his file for the hundredth time. He was missing something, he realized. That cold-blooded instinct for the kill.

He wasn't enjoying this, wasn't even close to experiencing the satisfaction he gained bringing his opponents to his knees. Somewhere along the line he'd changed. He'd sensed something was different shortly after he'd met Savannah. Now there was no hiding his feelings. He'd lost it. Only, he wasn't sure what he'd found.

"Have you got a moment?" John Stackhouse stuck his head in Dash's office.

"Sure. What can I do for you?"

The senior partner was smiling ear to ear. "Would you mind stepping down to the meeting room?"

Dash's pulse accelerated wildly. The executive committee was meeting with the other senior partners that afternoon to make their recommendation for the appointment of the new senior partner.

"I got the position?" Dash asked hesitatingly.

"I think that would be a fair assessment," the older man said, slapping Dash across the shoulders. "It wasn't a hard decision, Dash. You're a fine attorney and an asset to this law firm."

A half hour later, Dash rushed out of the office and drove directly to Savannah's shop. As luck would have it, she was busy with a customer. He tried to be patient, tried to pretend he was some stranger off the street who'd casually strolled into her shop, mildly curious about the wedding business.

Savannah glared at him with wide, questioning eyes and he delighted in unnerving her by blowing her a kiss.

"When did you say the wedding was?" she asked the smartly dressed businesswoman who was leafing through a book of invitations.

"In December."

"You have plenty of time, but it's a good idea to set your budget now. I'll be happy to assist you in any way I can."

"I appreciate that," Dash heard the woman say.

Dash wandered to her desk and sorted through her mail. Without being obvious, Savannah walked over to where he was sitting, took the envelopes from him and gently slapped his hands. "Behave yourself," she said under her breath.

"I have a few extra expenses coming up," he said in a low whisper. "I was hoping you're doing well. I might need a loan."

"What expenses?" she asked in the same low voice.

"New stationery and the like."

"New stationery?" she repeated much louder.

Savannah's customer turned around abruptly. "I'm sorry," she said apologetically. "I was commenting on something my husband said."

The woman smiled graciously. "I thought you two must be married. I saw the way you looked at each other when he walked in the door."

Neither Dash nor Savannah responded.

Savannah started to walk away, when Dash caught her hand. It was the first time he'd purposely touched her since the morning following their wedding. Apparently the action caught her by surprise, because she turned abruptly around, her gaze seeking out his.

"I'm the new senior partner."

Savannah's eyes lit up with undisguised delight. "Dash, oh, Dash." She covered her mouth with her hands and blinked back tears. "Congratulations."

"If you don't mind, I'll come back another time with my fiancé," Savannah's customer said.

"I'm sorry," Savannah said, limping toward the woman.

"Don't apologize. Celebrate with your husband. You both deserve it." When she reached the front door she turned the sign to "Closed," winked at Dash and walked out of the store.

"When did you find out?" Savannah asked, rubbing her index finger beneath her eye.

"No more than thirty minutes ago. I thought we'd go out to dinner and celebrate."

"I . . . don't know what to say. I'm so happy for you."

"I'm happy, too." It was difficult not to take her in his arms. Damned difficult. He stood and walked away from her rather than break his self-imposed restriction.

"Where are you going?" Savannah asked, sounding perplexed.

"I need to keep my distance from you."

"Why?"

"Because I want to hold you so damned much, my arms ache."

Savannah broke into a smile bright enough to rival the sun. "I was just thinking the same thing," she said, opening her arms to him.

Chapter Twelve

Dash checked his wrist for the time, set aside the evening paper and hurried into the kitchen. It was his night to cook and he'd experimented with a new recipe. If anyone had told him he'd be hanging around a kitchen, fretting over elaborate recipes to tempt his wife, Dash would have stoutly denied such a thing could happen.

Marriage had done this to him, and to his surprise Dash wasn't complaining. He rather enjoyed their arrangement, especially now that they were on much friendlier terms. The tension had lessened considerably following the evening they'd celebrated his appointment as senior partner. It felt as if the barriers were gradually being lowered as he slowly gained Savannah's trust.

He was bent over the oven door when he heard Savannah come into the house. She'd called him at the office to let him know she'd be late, which had become something of a nightly occurrence.

"I'm home," she said, coming into the kitchen. She looked pale and worn-out. He'd never have guessed September would be such a busy month for weddings. Savannah had overbooked herself and had spread her time and energy much too thin. He'd resisted the urge to lecture her, although it'd been difficult.

"Your timing couldn't be better," he said, taking the sausage, cabbage and cheese casserole out of the oven and setting it on the counter. The scent of spicy meat filled the compact kitchen.

"That smells delicious," Savannah said, and Dash beamed proudly. He'd discovered somewhat to his surprise that he enjoyed cooking. Over the years he'd learned a culinary trick or two, creating a small repertoire of dinners. Nothing, however, that required an actual recipe. Now he found himself reading cookbooks on a regular basis.

"I've got the table set if you're ready to eat," he told her.

"You must have known I was starving."

"Did you skip lunch again today?" he asked, using oven mitts to carry the glass casserole dish to the table. Once again he had to stop himself from chastising her. Their peace was too fragile to test. "Sit down and I'll bring you a plate."

It looked as if Savannah was in danger of falling asleep as he joined her at the table.

"Dash," she said after the first taste, "this is wonderful."

"I'm glad you approve."

"Keep this up and you can do all the cooking," she teased, gently smiling over at him. It was the kind of smile a man would gladly walk across a bed of nails to receive. The edges of her mouth moved upward at just the right angle to say how very happy she was. Dash reluctantly pulled his gaze from her, thinking he was behaving like a lovesick bull.

He set his fork aside and folded his hands. He couldn't keep silent any longer. "You're working too hard."

She lowered her gaze and nodded. "I know. I scheduled the majority of these weddings soon after our own. I...I thought it would be a good idea if I spent as much time at the shop as possible."

In other words, less time with him. "I hope you've changed your mind since then."

"I have." Her hand closed around her water glass. "I assumed our...arrangement would be awkward and uneasy, but it hasn't been, other than at the beginning."

"I've enjoyed spending time with you." It frustrated the hell out of him, living as they did, like polite strangers, but that, too, had changed in the past couple of weeks. Their relationship had altered to that of good friends. Their progress was slow but steady, and that gave Dash hope that eventually Savannah would be comfortable enough with him to make love. He realized his attitude was shortsighted. Cracking that barrier had been a challenge from the first, but he hadn't thought beyond that. He didn't want to think about it now.

When they finished eating, Savannah carried their plates to the sink. They had an agreement about cleanup, one of many understandings. When one did the cooking, the other washed the dishes.

"Sit down," Dash ordered, "before you collapse."

"This will only take a couple of minutes," she insisted, opening the dishwasher.

Dash took her by the hands and led her into the living room. Placing pressure on her shoulders, he forced her onto the davenport. "I want you to relax."

"If I do that, I'll fall asleep, and I need to go back to the shop later and finish up a few things."

"Don't even think about it, Savannah. I won't allow it." Those were fighting words, but he counted on her being much too tired to argue with him. "You're exhausted. I'm your husband, and I may not be a very good one, but I refuse to allow you to work yourself this hard."

She closed her eyes and leaned her head against the thick sofa cushion. She gave him a small smile. "You're a good husband, Dash. Thoughtful and considerate."

"Right." He hoped she wasn't expecting an argument. As it was, he should be awarded some kind of medal. He was convinced heaven had it in for him, otherwise he wouldn't be forced to live with this delectable, desirable woman and not make love to her.

He reached for her legs, and placed them on his lap. "Just relax," he urged when she opened her eyes, silently questioning him. He removed her shoes and slowly massaged her tired feet. She sighed with pleasure and wiggled her toes.

"I haven't been to my place in a week," she said, and Dash found that to be an odd comment until he thought about it. She was admitting how comfortable she'd gotten living with him. It was a sign, a small one, that she was willing to advance their relationship. Dash didn't intend on wasting it.

"I've moved nearly all my clothes here," she continued in sleepy tones.

"That's very good, don't you think?" he asked, not expecting her to reply.

"Hmm."

He continued to rub her feet and ankles, marveling at the delicate bone structure. He found the action mildly erotic and allowed his hands to venture upward over her calves. She sighed and nestled farther down in the sofa. Gaining confidence, Dash risked going higher, where her skin was silky warm and smooth. He wasn't sure how this was affecting Savannah, but it was having a strong, curious effect on him. His breathing went shallow and his heart started to thunder in his ears. He'd promised himself, swore before all that was holy, that he wouldn't ask her to make love again. She would have to come to him. He wanted her to beg for all the frustration she'd put him through this past month. But if anyone was going to do any begging, it was him.

"It's very relaxing," Savannah murmured with a sigh.

Funny, it had the opposite effect on him. He was already hard. So hard that he hurt. He dared not let Savannah know how strongly this was affecting him.

Her skin was like satin, soft and pliable. He ran his hands along the inside of both thighs, reaching as high as he dared go, damning himself for not going farther.

"Dash." His name was released on a harshly indrawn breath.

His hands froze. His heart went still and his breath caught in his throat until his lungs hurt. "Yes?" He struggled to sound expressionless, although heaven knew it was near impossible. The less she recognized how critical his need was for her, the better, although there was no hiding the hardened bulge in his pants.

"I think I should stop, don't you?" Where he dredged up the mettle to suggest that was beyond him.

"It feels good."

"That's the problem. It feels too damn good."

"For you, too?"

Sometimes he forgot what an innocent she was. "For me, too."

Her head was propped against the back of the sofa, her eyes closed. Her mouth was slightly parted and she moistened her lips with the tip of her tongue. Dash groaned inwardly and forced himself to look away.

"Maybe we should kiss," she offered, sounding none too sure.

Dash wasn't looking for a repeat performance of what had taken place earlier, but at the same time he wasn't about to turn down her offer. She wasn't begging, but this was close enough.

He shifted his weight, brought her into his arms and was about to lower his mouth to hers with anticipation so keen, he felt as if he would explode if she so much as moved.

Perspiration broke out across his brow and he held his breath while he reined in his desire. "If we start kissing, we might not be able to stop."

"I know."

"You know that?" Something was wrong with him. Very wrong. He should be carrying her into the bedroom and not ask questions until afterward. A long time afterward. Perhaps never.

"We can follow through with our agreement, can't we?" she asked. Her eyes fluttered open.

"What agreement?" His mind was like a sieve, only able to hold one thing, and at the moment that was his painful physical need for her.

"We'll maintain separate residences once my parents decide to travel," she said, and it sounded more like a reassurance. "I'm not going to be trapped in a loveless marriage."

"Fine," he said, willing to agree to any terms. "Whatever you want."

"Do you think it would be a mistake to make love?"

"No." He intended to shout, but the lone word came out sounding as if he'd choked on something. "That sounds like a very good idea to me," he said a couple of seconds later, managing to appear perfectly normal. He climbed off the davenport, reached down and scooted her into his arms.

She gave a small cry of surprise when he lifted her off the davenport and marched down the darkened hallway. He walked into his bedroom and placed her on his bed. It was where she belonged and where she would stay from this night forward.

He was afraid of hurting her, he realized, afraid of going too fast, of not going fast enough. Afraid of not lasting long enough, of cheating her out of what lovemaking should be for her first time. His fears managed to wrap strong cords of indecision around him.

"Is something wrong?" she asked, staring up at him in the dark, her eyes wide and questioning.

Unable to answer, he shook his head.

She smiled then, softly, femininely, and stretched her arms up to him, bringing him down next to her. He noticed that her breathing was as quick and shallow as his own and that went a long ways toward consoling him. Carefully he peeled open the front of her shirt and eased it from her shoulders. Her bra and everything else soon followed. Her nipples were tight even before he touched them, and they grew even stiffer when he rubbed his hands over their plump contours. Her eyes were half-closed as he created a new kind of pleasure for her to enjoy. The pleasure of anticipation.

She moaned even before his mouth closed over her nipple. He sucked strong and hard and she buckled, naked beneath him. The anticipation was doing dangerous things to him, as well. He needed to be inside her and if it didn't happen soon, Dash was convinced he'd go mad.

He knew he had to stop now and remove his clothes or it would be over within seconds. She moaned in protest when he rolled off her, and raised herself up on one elbow while he hurriedly undressed. He jerked back his belt so hard, he nearly choked off his breath. The zipper sounded like a buzz saw in the silence as he released his pants and let them drop to the floor. He was kicking them free of his feet while he worked his tie and shirt free of the fasteners. Growing impatient, he jerked it off his head and tossed it aside; only God knew or cared where it landed.

Soon he stood naked, except for his socks, which he was clumsily struggling to remove. Savannah apparently enjoyed the show because she was smiling up at him warmly. Her smile waned slightly as it rested on his throbbing shaft.

"Don't look so worried," he said, joining her on the bed once again.

"I'm not," she said, and it was plain to him she'd lied. He kissed her several times until they were both panting. It was necessary to stop, necessary for his sanity. He couldn't wait a moment longer, and prayed this wasn't too soon for her.

As carefully as he could, he shifted her weight, poised himself above her and guided himself slowly, inch by incredible inch, inside his wife. When he'd reached as far as he dared, he paused, giving her a moment to adjust to this invasion of her body.

Savannah's hands gripped the sheets on either side of her as her breasts heaved with several deep breaths. Her eyes were squeezed shut.

"Am I hurting you?"

"No... it feels good."

The tip of his manhood pressed against her feminine barrier. He'd never been more uncertain about anything. If he proceeded, he'd cause her pain; if he stopped now, he'd likely go insane himself.

Savannah must have read his indecision because she relaxed her shoulders and raised her hands to his face, tracing the outline of his jaw, her cool fingertips just grazing his heated skin, creating a new realm of sensation. "Don't look so worried. You're about to make me a woman."

Closing her eyes, she sighed, braced her hands against his shoulders and arched her hips upward with a swift, bold motion. The obstruction was gone with such ease that Dash was sure there was some mistake.

"You're all right?" he asked, half-panicked.

"Yes, oh, yes."

He moved and felt her expand to accommodate him. Waves of hot pleasure rippled out though his body and he increased the tempo. He could feel his climax approach like a runaway freight train. There was no stopping it, no slowing its progress, no diverting it from its course. He tried desperately to hold back but it was beyond his human strength, beyond his capabilities. With a wild shout of triumph he spilled his seed.

Savannah was whimpering softly and his immediate concern was that he'd injured her in some way, hurt this woman who had given so unselfishly of herself. He spread kisses over her face, all the while telling her how sorry he was.

She wrapped her arms around his neck and eagerly accepted his mouth, making soft, unintelligible sounds. She wasn't in pain; that much he could tell. If anything, she seemed to be joyously happy. That seemed a miracle to him.

They fell asleep like that, their arms and legs intertwined, their bodies joined in the most elemental of ways. Dash had never known such peace, never experienced such serenity, and it lulled him into a deep sleep.

It was after midnight when Dash woke. The lights were still on in the living room and the kitchen. Carefully, so not to wake Savannah, he crawled out of the bed and reached for his robe. Shuffling barefoot out of the bedroom, he covered his mouth and yawned.

He felt good. Damn good. Like he could run a marathon or swim a mile in world-record time. He finished what there was of the dinner dishes and was turning off the kitchen light when he looked up and saw Savannah standing just inside the living room.

Her hair was tousled, yet he couldn't ever remember seeing her look more beautiful, other than on their wedding day. For prudence' sake she'd donned her blouse, which covered precious little of her ripe, young body.

"I woke and you were gone," she said, sounding like a child who was afraid of a storm.

"I was coming back to bed."

"Good." She led the way, not that he required any coaxing. He may have been a lot of things, but for this one night, he was no fool. The room was dark, but streaks of moonlight floated against the wall as they made their way back to the bed.

Dash held back the covers and Savannah climbed onto the mattress. Dash followed, gathering her in his arms, cradling her head against his shoulder. She lay on her side, her breasts cushioning his chest, her leg looped over his.

He waited for her to speak, wondering what she was thinking, afraid to ask. Her hair smelled of roses and sunshine. With utter contentment he kissed the crown of her head. She squirmed against him, nestling in as close as humanly possible, and released a long, womanly sigh.

Although he was an experienced lover, Dash had never heard a woman sigh the way Savannah did just then. It seemed to come from deep in her lungs and it poured out of her like warm honey, speaking of expected pleasure and the surprise of mutual satisfaction.

His throat felt as if there was an obstruction blocking it. His breathing became heavy as emotion settled over him like a hard rock.

"Thank you," he whispered when he could.

"No," she corrected, "thank you." And then she snuggled up to him once more, as if she needed this closeness as much as he did. As if she craved, as if she needed, these peace-filled moments the same as he.

He waited a few more moments, wanting to be sure she hadn't drifted off to sleep. "This changes things."

"I know," she whispered with a tinge of regret. "I thought about it long and hard before we made love."

"Oh?"

"I planned on talking it over with you, discussing details, reassessing the issues, that sort of thing."

"Why didn't you?" He couldn't help but be curious.

He felt her lips move into a gentle smile. "When the time came, all I wanted was you."

His chest rose with an abundance of fierce male pride. "I wanted you, too."

This was what heaven must be like, Dash decided. Serenity surrounded him and he sank into its warm, protective folds.

"Don't you think we should talk?" Savannah asked after a moment.

"About what?" He was perfectly content just the way matters were.

"Us, I guess," she whispered, sounding hesitant.

The last thing Dash wanted now was a lengthy discussion of the different aspects of their marriage. Words were sure to destroy the tranquillity, and these moments were too precious to waste.

"This doesn't have to change anything, if you don't want it to," Dash murmured, rubbing his chin over the top of her head, loving the way her silky hair felt against his skin.

Savannah went still and he wondered if he'd sai
something wrong. "You're content with our arrang
ment the way it is?" she asked.

"For now I am. We don't have to make any dec
sions tonight, do we?"

"No," she agreed readily.

"Then relax and go back to sleep." His eyes drift
shut and he moved his hand up and down the leng
of her arm, savoring this closeness.

"Dash." She sounded hesitant again, unsure
herself.

"Hmm?"

"Would you . . . can I touch you?" Her arm w
draped over his midsection, and at his nod she slipp
her hand onto his abdomen and slowly lowered
pausing when she reached the heat of his strength. S
seemed wary, uncertain, and he smiled, enjoying h
hesitation and her willingness to investigate his ph
sique with newfound freedom.

"It was nothing like what I expected," she told hi
softly.

"Better, I hope."

"Oh, yes." Her fingers closed around him then, h
touch light, tentative. His response was precisely t
opposite. His head came up off the thick folds of h
pillow and he sucked in a deep breath.

"Savannah," he warned between clenched teeth.

"Yes?" she asked innocently. Her touch gain
significant confidence as she stroked the length of h
throbbing erection.

He answered her the only way he could, by car
fully moving over her. The suddenness of his r
sponse caused her to gasp and then softly laugh. B

instead of her pulling her hand away, as he'd expected, she stroked him more.

"You think this is funny, do you?" he asked, barely able to speak as the pleasure of her sensuous touch washed over him.

"Hilarious."

"We'll see what you have to say about it in about two seconds."

"Yes, oh, yes." She kissed his throat and covered his buttocks with her flattened palms as he eased himself into her. She gasped a second time, but the sound radiated not with surprise, but with sheer pleasure. Dear, sweet heaven, she was tight and moist and smooth and he was about to lose his mind for want of her. Above everything else, she was his. The richest prize of all. His wife. His lover. His friend.

Don and Janice Griffin's meeting before Judge Wilcox was scheduled for two in the afternoon. Dash was well prepared for this finalization of the divorce proceedings.

Don Griffin arrived at his office an hour early and in what was fast becoming a habit, set to pacing the confines of the room. It was a wonder he hadn't worn a pattern in the carpet.

"I'm ready any time you are," his client insisted.

"If we leave now, we'll end up sitting outside in the hallway," Dash told him.

"That's fine. I want this over with as quickly and cleanly as possible, understand?"

"That message came through loud and clear from the first," Dash assured him. "Settle down and relax, will you?"

Don thrust the fingers of both hands into his ha
and held on. "Relax? Are you crazy, man? You migh
have gone through this a thousand times, but this i
almost thirty years of my life we're throwing out th
window. If you're going to amputate both arms an
one leg, I'd rather get it over with than sit through on
more day of constant dread."

"What's this I hear about you putting a divorc
special on your restaurant's menu?" Dash asked in a
effort to take the older man's mind off the comin
proceedings. "Anyone who comes into any one c
your restaurants the day his divorce is final eats free.'

"That's right, and I'd rather you didn't say any
thing derogatory about it. I've met a handful of me
just like me. Some married twenty, thirty years and a
of a sudden it's gone. Poof. Suddenly they're lost an
alone and they don't know what the hell to do with th
rest of their lives."

"I'm not going to say anything negative. I think it'
a generous thing you're doing."

Don Griffin eyed him as if he wasn't sure he shoul
believe him.

When they arrived at the courtroom, Mr. Griffi
and Dash took their seats behind one table. Janic
Griffin and Tony Pound sat behind the other. Das
noticed the way Don stole a look at his very-soon-to
be ex-wife. Next, he caught a glimpse of Janice look
ing at Don. It wasn't anything he hadn't seen coun
less times before. One last look, so to speak, before th
ties were severed. A farewell. An acceptance that it wa
soon to be over—the end was within sight. This mar
riage was about to breathe its last breath.

Judge Wilcox entered the room and everyone stoo
With a crisp, businesslike attitude, a series of ques

ions were asked of each party. Janice responded, her
hin voice wavering. Don answered sounding like a
condemned man. They stood, sat back down and the
inal decree was about to be pronounced when Dash
aulted out of his seat.

For a moment he didn't know what had forced him
nto action. "If you'll pardon me, Your Honor,"
Dash said, with his back to his client, "I'd like to say
a few words."

He could hear Tony rise to his feet in automatic ob-
ection. Dash didn't give him the opportunity.

"My client doesn't want this divorce, and neither
does his wife."

A string of hot words erupted behind him as Tony
Pound flew out of his chair. The judge's gavel
ounded several times, the noise deafening.

"Your Honor, if you'll indulge me for just a moment."

No one was more surprised than Dash when he was
iven permission. "Proceed."

"My client has been married for almost thirty years.
He made a mistake, Your Honor. Now, he'll be the
irst to admit it was a foolish, stupid mistake. But he's
uman and so is his wife. They've both paid dearly for
his blunder and it seems to me they've paid enough."

He turned to face Janice Griffin, who was gripping
a tissue in her hand as if it were a lifeline. "You've
made mistakes in your life, too, haven't you, Mrs.
Griffin?"

Janice lowered her gaze and nodded.

"You can't cross-examine my client," Pound
houted.

Dash ignored him, and thankfully so did Judge
Wilcox.

"My client has loved his wife and family for near thirty years. He loves her still. I saw the way he looke at Mrs. Griffin when she walked into the courtroom I also saw the way she looked at him. These two pe ple care deeply for each other. They've been drive apart by their pain and their pride. Nearly thirty yea is a very long time out of a person's life. I don't b lieve anyone should be in a rush to just sign it away.

"Your Honor, I find this outburst extremely u professional," Tony Pound protested.

Dash didn't dare turn around and face him.

"Don Griffin has suffered enough for his indiscr tion. Mrs. Griffin has been through enough agon too. It's time to think about building lives instead destroying them."

There wasn't a sound in the courtroom. Having ha his say, Dash returned to his seat.

Judge Wilcox held on to his gavel with both hand "Is what Mr. Davenport said true, Mr. Griffin? D you love your wife?"

Don Griffin slowly rose to his feet. "A thousan times more than I thought was possible."

"Mrs. Griffin?"

She, too, stood, her eyes watering, her lips tren bling. "Yes, Your Honor."

The judge glared at them both and set the gavel rest. "Then I suggest you try to reconcile your diffe ences and stop wasting the court's time."

Dash gathered together the papers he'd remove from his briefcase and set them back inside. Do Griffin walked behind him and was met halfway by h wife. From his peripheral vision, Dash watched Janice Griffin, sobbing, walked into her husband

rms. The two held on to each other, weeping and
aughing and kissing all at once.

It wasn't bad for an afternoon's work, Dash de-
ided.

Dash took his briefcase and walked out of the
ourtroom. He hadn't taken two steps when Tony
'ound joined him.

"That was quite a little drama you put on just
ow."

"I couldn't see two people who were obviously in
ove with each other end their marriage," Dash said.
'heir steps made clicking sounds against the marble
loors as they marched like twin soldiers through the
rogressive hallways of justice.

"It's true, then," Tony commented.

"What is?"

"That you've lost your edge, that killer instinct
ou're famous for. I have to admit I'm glad to see it.
'eople said it'd happen as soon as they learned you'd
larried, but no one expected it would be this soon.
Vhoever took you on as a husband must be one hell
f a woman."

Dash smiled to himself. "She is."

"It doesn't look like I'll be seeing you in court all
lat often."

"Probably not. I'm not taking on any new divorce
ases."

"Dad, what an unexpected surprise," Savannah
lid, delighted her father had decided to drop in un-
xpectedly at her shop. He didn't often visit and his
ming was perfect. She was about to take a break, sit
own and rest her leg. "How's Mom?"

"Much better," he said, pulling out a chair as Savannah poured him a cup of coffee.

"Good."

"That's what I've come to talk to you about."

Savannah poured herself a cup and joined him. H mother had made phenomenal progress in the past s weeks. Savannah made a point of calling and visitin often. Joyce's voice was growing stronger each da She was often forgetful and that frustrated her, b otherwise she was recuperating nicely.

"I thought it'd be a good idea if I talked to y first," her father said.

"About what?"

"Your mother and I traveling."

It was the welcome news she'd been waiting to hea At the same time it was the dreaded announceme that would end the happiest days of her life.

"I think you should travel. I always have."

"I was hoping to take your mother south. We mig even look for a place to buy."

"Arizona," she suggested, holding the cup to h lips. "Mom's always loved the Southwest."

"The sunshine will do her a world of good," h father agreed.

Savannah didn't know how she was able to pull th off, when she felt like she was dying on the insid Over the years she'd gotten incredibly good at di guising her pain. Pain made others uncomfortable a so she'd learned to live with it, better than she'd re ized.

"You wouldn't object to our going?" Her fath didn't often sound hesitant but he did so now.

"Of course I don't. I want you to travel, and enjoy your retirement years. I've got Dash now so there's no need to worry about me. None whatsoever."

"You're sure?"

"Dad! Go and enjoy yourselves," Savannah said and laughed, which was another minor miracle.

Three hours later, Savannah sat in the middle of Dash's living room, staring aimlessly into space. All that was left now was the interminable waiting.

Dash arrived home shortly after six. His eyes were triumphant as he marched into the house. "Savannah," he said, sounding delighted to see her. "You didn't work late tonight."

"No," she responded simply.

He lifted her off the sofa as if she weighed nothing more than a few pounds and twirled her around. "I had the most incredible day."

"Me, too."

"Good. We'll celebrate." Tucking his arm beneath her knees, he started for the bedroom. He stopped abruptly when he spied her suitcase sitting at the end of the hallway. His eyes were filled with unasked questions as they met hers.

"Are you going somewhere?"

She nodded. "My parents have decided to take an extended trip south."

"So?"

"So, according to the terms of our marriage agreement, I'm moving back into my own home."

Chapter Thirteen

"You're moving out just like that?" Dash asked, lowering her feet to the ground. He stepped away from her as if it was essential to put some distance between them. His gaze narrowed and he studied her as if he was seeing her with new eyes.

Savannah hadn't expected him to look at her as if he was shocked. This was what they'd decided in the beginning, it was what he said he wanted after they'd made love the first time a week earlier. She'd asked, wanting to be clear on exactly what place she was to have in his life, and Dash had specifically stated that their making love changed nothing.

"This shouldn't come as a surprise," she said stiffly, struggling to keep her voice as even as possible.

"Is it what you want?" He buried his hands deep inside his pants pockets and glared icily at her. In the time she'd known Dash, she recognized several aspects of his personality that made him an excellent attorney. She added *the look* to the list. His eyes seemed capable of cutting straight through her.

"Well?" he demanded when she didn't answer right away.

"It doesn't matter what I think. I'm holding up my end of the bargain. What do you want me to do?"

Dash gave a nonchalant shrug of his shoulders. "I'm not going to hold you prisoner here against your wishes, if that's what you're asking."

What she was asking was for some indication that he loved her and wanted her living with him. Some indication that he intended to throw out their stupid prenuptial agreement and make this marriage as real as she'd prayed. Apparently Dash wasn't interested.

"When are your parents leaving?"

"Friday morning, at dawn."

"So soon?"

She nodded. "Dad wanted to wait until Mom was strong enough to travel comfortably... and evidently she is now. They've been talking about driving to Arizona for some time, but only recently decided to go ahead with their plans."

"I see." Dash wandered into the kitchen. "So you're planning to move out right away?"

"I... thought I'd take a load of clothes over to my house this evening."

"You certainly seem to be in a rush."

"Not really. I've managed to accumulate quite a bit of my personal items here. I... imagine you'll want me out of your hair as quickly as possible." The most infinitesimal sign he loved her would be enough to convince her to stay. A simple statement of needing her. A word. A look. Anything.

Dash offered nothing.

He opened the refrigerator and took out a cold soda. The can made a popping sound when he opened it and tiny, fizzing bubbles appeared at the top.

"I put dinner on while I was waiting for you," she said. "The pork chops are warming in the oven."

Dash took a long swallow of the soda. "I appreciate the effort, but I don't seem to have much of an appetite."

Savannah didn't, either. Calmly she walked over and turned off the oven. She stood with her back to Dash and bit into her lower lip.

What a romantic fool she was, looking for the impossible to happen. She'd known when she agreed to marry Dash that it would be like this. He was going to break her heart. She'd attempted protective measures to guard herself from exactly this, but they hadn't done any good.

These past few weeks had been the happiest of her life and nothing he said now would take them away from her. He loved her, she knew it, as much as it was possible for Dash to care about someone. He'd never said the words, but he didn't need to. She felt them when she slept in his arms. She experienced them each time they made love.

Her heart constricted with fresh pain. She didn't want to leave Dash, but she couldn't stay, not unless he specifically asked it of her, and it was clear he had no intention of doing so.

She heard him leave the room, which was just as well since she was having a damnable time not breaking into tears.

She was angry then, damned angry. Unfortunately there wasn't a door to slam or anything handy to throw. Having a temper tantrum was exactly what she felt like doing.

Dinner was a waste. She might as well throw the whole thing in the garbage. Opening the oven door, she reached inside and grabbed hold of the pan.

Intense, unexpected pain shot through her fingers as her bare skin touched the baking dish.

She cried out with the shock of it and jerked her hand away. Stumbling toward the sink, she immediately placed her fingers under cold running water, holding her hand by the wrist.

"Savannah?" Dash rushed back into the kitchen. "What happened?"

"I'm all right," she said, fighting back tears by taking in deep breaths. If she was lucky, her fingers wouldn't blister, but she seemed to be plumb out of good fortune lately.

"What happened?" Dash demanded.

"Nothing." She shook her head, not wanting to answer him because doing so required concentration and effort, and all she could think of at the moment was pain. Physical pain. Emotional agony. The two had intermingled until she didn't know where one stopped and the other started.

"Let me look at what you've done," he said, scooting next to her.

"No," Savannah argued, jerking her arm away from him. "It's nothing."

"Let me be the judge of that."

"Leave me alone," she cried, sobbing openly now, her shoulders heaving. "Just leave me be. I can take care of myself."

"I'm your husband."

She whirled on him then, unintentionally splashing him with cold water. "How can you say that when you can hardly wait to be rid of me?"

"What the hell are you talking about?" he shouted. "I wasn't the one who packed my bags and casually announced I was leaving. If you want to throw out a few questions, then you might start asking yourself what kind of wife you are!"

Savannah rubbed the back of her good hand beneath her nose. "You claimed you didn't want a wife."

"I didn't until I married you." Dash opened the freezer portion of the refrigerator and brought out the tub of ice cubes. "Sit down," he said in tones that brooked no argument. She complied. He set the ice on the table and gently placed her burned fingers in the filled tub. "The first couple of minutes will be the most uncomfortable, but after that you won't feel anything," he explained calmly.

Savannah continued to sob softly; the sounds were like a mild case of the hiccups. Her shoulders jerked up and down with the action.

"What did you do?" he asked a second time.

"I reached for the baking dish."

Dash frowned. "Did the mitt slip?"

"I forgot to use one," she admitted reluctantly.

He took a moment to digest this information before kneeling down on the floor at her feet. His eyes probed hers and she lowered her gaze. Tucking his finger beneath her chin, he leveled her eyes with his.

"Why?" he asked.

"Isn't it obvious? I . . . was upset."

"About what?"

She shrugged, not wanting to admit the truth. "These things happen and . . ."

"Why?" he repeated softly.

"Because you're an idiot," she flared.

"I know you're upset about me not wanting to eat dinner, but—"

"Dinner?" she cried, incredulous. "You think this is because you don't feel like dinner? How can any man be so incredibly dense?" It was too much to think about while sitting. She vaulted to her feet, her burned fingers forgotten. "You were going to let me just walk out of here."

"Wrong."

"Wrong? And just how did you plan to stop me?"

"I figured I'd move in with you."

She blinked. "I beg your pardon."

"You heard me right. The agreement, as it was originally written, stated you'll move out of my premises after your parents had decided to travel and you—"

"I know what that stupid piece of paper says," Savannah said, frowning.

"If you didn't want to live with me, then it made perfect sense for me to take measures into my own hands."

"I do want to live with you, you idiot," she cried, rubbing her good hand down her face. "I was hoping you'd do something—anything—to convince me to stay."

Dash was quiet for a moment. "Let me see if I have this straight. You were going to move out, although you didn't want to. Is that right?"

She nodded.

"Why?"

"Because I wanted you to ask me to stay."

"Ah, I understand now. You do one thing, hoping I'll respond another way."

She shrugged, realizing how incredibly stupid it all sounded in the harsh light of reason. "Something like that."

"Let this be a lesson to you, Savannah Daven-port," Dash said, taking her in his arms. "If you want something, all you need to do is ask for it. If you'd simply sought my opinion on your leaving, you'd have learned something."

"Oh?"

"I'm willing to move heaven and hell to make sure we're together the rest of our natural lives."

"You are?"

"In case you haven't figured it out yet, I'm in love with you." A surprised look must have come over her face because he added, "You honestly didn't know?"

"I...prayed you were, but I didn't dare hope you'd admit it. I've been in love with you for so long that I can't remember when I didn't love you."

He kissed her gently, his mouth coaxing and warm. "Promise me you won't ever stop loving me. I need you so badly. It wasn't until you were in my life that I realized how jaded I'd become. Taking on the divorce cases didn't help my attitude any. I've made a decision recently that's due to your influence on me. When I first graduated from law school, I specialized in tax and tax laws. I'm going back to that."

"Oh, Dash, I'm so pleased."

He kissed her with a hunger that left her weak and clinging.

"I can ask for anything?" she murmured between kisses.

"Anything."

"Throw away that stupid agreement."

He smiled boyishly and pressed his forehead against hers. "I already have.... The first night, after we'd made love."

"You might have told me."

"I intended to when the time was right."

"And when did you calculate that to be?" she asked, having a difficult time maintaining her feigned outrage.

"Soon, very soon."

She smiled and closed her eyes. "Apparently not soon enough."

"I had high hopes for us from the first. I opened my mouth and stuck my foot in it from the beginning by suggesting that stupid marriage-of-convenience idea. Marriage, the second time around, is a hell of a lot more frightening after you've made one mistake."

"Our marriage isn't a mistake," she assured him. "I won't let it be."

"I felt if I had control of the situation, I might be able to manage my feelings for you, but the minute I saw you at the wedding I knew that was going to be impossible."

"Why didn't you follow your own advice and ask?" she said, thinking of all the weeks they'd wasted.

"We didn't seem to be on the best of terms afterward, if you'll remember."

Savannah was embarrassed now by what a shrew she'd been. She looped her arms around his neck and kissed him soundly in an effort to make up for those first few weeks.

"You said I can ask for anything I want?" she said against his lips.

"Hmm . . . anything," he agreed.

"I'd very much like a baby."

Dash's eyes flew open with undisguised eagerness. "How soon?"

"Well . . . I was thinking we could start on the project tonight."

A slow, lazy smile came into place. "That's a very good idea, very good indeed."

* * *

"I can't believe the changes in Dash," Susan commented. Kurt and Susan had flown up from California to spend the Christmas holiday with them this year. The two women were busily working in the kitchen.

"He's such a good father to Jacob," Savannah said, blinking back unexpected tears. She cried so easily when she was pregnant and she was entering her second trimester with this baby. If the ultrasound was accurate, they were going to have a little girl.

"Dash is doing so well and so are you. Don't you miss working at the shop?"

"No, I've got a wonderful manager and you can't imagine how busy a fourteen-month-old keeps me. I've thought about going back part-time and then decided not to, not now at any rate. What about you? Will you continue teaching?" Savannah softly patted Susan's slightly distended stomach.

"Probably not, but I'll probably work on a substitute basis to keep my credentials up so when our family's complete, I can return without a lot of hassle."

"That's smart."

"She's my sister, isn't she?" Dash said, walking into the kitchen, cradling his son in his arms. Jacob gibbered, happily waving his rattle in every which direction. He'd been a happy baby from the first. Their joy.

Kurt's arms surrounded his wife and he flattened his hands over Susan's stomach. "We've decided to have our two close together, the way you and Savannah have planned your family."

Savannah and Dash exchanged smiles. "Planned?" she teased her husband.

"The operative word there is *two*," Dash said, eyeing her suspiciously.

"Sweetheart, we've been over this a hundred times. I really would like four children."

"Four!" Dash cried. "The last time we talked you said you'd be content with three."

"I've changed my mind. Four is a nice, even number."

"Four children is out of the question," Dash said with a disgruntled look, then seemed to notice Kurt and Susan staring at him. "We'll talk about this later, all right, but we will talk."

"Of course we will," Savannah promised, unable to hold back a smile.

"She's going to do it," Dash grumbled to his sister and brother-in-law. "She knows I can't refuse her anything. Somehow before I've figured out how she's managed it, we'll be a family of six."

"You'll love it, Dash, I promise." The oven timer rang and Savannah glanced at the clock. "Oh, dear, I've got to get busy. Mr. Sterle and Mr. Stackhouse will be here any minute."

"This is something else she didn't tell me before we were married," Dash said, his eyes shining with love. "She collects people the way others do stray animals."

"They love Jacob," Savannah reminded him.

Dash laughed and shook his head. "I've never seen two old men more taken with a toddler."

"I don't think I've ever seen a man more taken with his wife," Susan added. "I could almost be jealous, but there isn't any need." She looped her arms around Kurt's neck. "Still, it doesn't do any harm to keep him on his toes."

"No, it doesn't," Savannah agreed.

* * * * *

Share in the joy of a holiday romance with

1993
SILHOUETTE

Christmas

STORIES

Silhouette's eighth annual
Christmas collection
matches the joy of the
holiday season with the
magic of romance in four
short stories by popular
Silhouette authors:

**LISA JACKSON
EMILIE RICHARDS
JOAN HOHL
LUCY GORDON**

This November, come home
for the holidays with

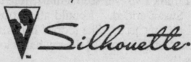

where passion lives.

SX93

**And now for
something completely different
from Silhouette....**

SPELLBOUND
R O M A N C E

Every once in a while, Silhouette brings you a book that is truly unique and innovative, taking you into the world of paranormal happenings. And now these stories will carry our special "Spellbound" flash, letting you know that you're in for a truly exciting reading experience!

In October, look for *McLain's Law* (IM #528) by Kylie Brant

Lieutenant Detective Connor McLain believes only in what he can see—until Michele Easton's haunting visions help him solve a case...and her love opens his heart!

McLain's Law is also the Intimate Moments "Premiere" title, introducing you to a debut author, sure to be the star of tomorrow!

Available in October...only from Silhouette Intimate Moments

SPELL1

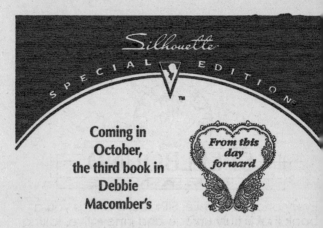

Silhouette

SPECIAL EDITION

Coming in
October,
the third book in
Debbie
Macomber's

From this day forward

MARRIAGE WANTED

Dash Davenport didn't marry Savannah Charles for love, only convenience.
As a divorce attorney, he knew marriage was a mistake. But as a man, Dash
couldn't resist Savannah's charms. It seemed Savannah knew all the makings
of a happily-ever-after. And it wasn't long after saying "I do" that Dash
started thinking about forever....

FROM THIS DAY FORWARD—Three couples marry first and
find love later in this heartwarming trilogy.

Only from Silhouette Special Edition.

If you missed *Groom Wanted* (SE #831) or *Bride Wanted* (SE #836), order your copy
now by sending your name, address, zip or postal code, along with a check or money
order (please do not send cash) for $3.50 plus 75¢ postage and handling ($1.00 in
Canada), payable to Silhouette Books, to:

In the U.S.	In Canada
Silhouette Books	Silhouette Books
3010 Walden Ave.	P. O. Box 636
P. O. Box 9077	Fort Erie, Ontario
Buffalo, NY 14269-9077	L2A 5X3

Please specify book title(s) with your order.
Canadian residents add applicable federal and provincial taxes.

SETD-

Premiere

Silhouette Books has done it again!

Opening night in October has never been as exciting! Come watch as the curtain rises and romance flourishes when the stars of tomorrow make their debuts today!

Revel in Jodi O'Donnell's STILL SWEET ON HIM—
Silhouette Romance #969
...as Callie Farrell's renovation of the family homestead leads her straight into the arms of teenage crush Drew Barnett!

Tingle with Carol Devine's BEAUTY AND THE BEASTMASTER—
Silhouette Desire #816
...as legal eagle Amanda Tarkington is carried off by wrestler Bram Masterson!

Thrill to Elyn Day's A BED OF ROSES—
Silhouette Special Edition #846
...as Dana Whitaker's body and soul are healed by sexy physical therapist Michael Gordon!

Believe when Kylie Brant's McLAIN'S LAW —
Silhouette Intimate Moments #528
...takes you into detective Connor McLain's life as he falls for psychic—and suspect—Michele Easton!

Catch the classics of tomorrow—*premiering* today—
only from ▼ *Silhouette*

PREM

If you're looking for more titles by

DEBBIE MACOMBER,

don't miss these heartwarming stories by one of
Silhouette's most popular authors:

Silhouette Special Edition®

#09662	NAVY BRAT	$3.25 ☐
#09683	NAVY WOMAN	$3.25 ☐
#09697	NAVY BABY	$3.29 ☐
#09744	STAND-IN WIFE+	$3.39 ☐
#09756	BRIDE ON THE LOOSE+	$3.39 ☐
#09798	HASTY WEDDING	$3.39 ☐
#09831	GROOM WANTED*	$3.50 ☐
#09836	BRIDE WANTED*	$3.50 ☐

+Those Manning Men
*From This Day Forward

Silhouette® Books

#45152	BORROWED DREAMS	$3.59 ☐
	(Men Made in America series—Alaska)	
#48254	TO MOTHER WITH LOVE '93	$4.99 ☐
	(short-story collection also featuring Diana Palmer and Judith Duncan)	

TOTAL AMOUNT	$
POSTAGE & HANDLING	$
($1.00 for one book, 50¢ for each additional)	
APPLICABLE TAXES**	$ _____
TOTAL PAYABLE	$ _____
(check or money order—please do not send cash)	

To order, complete this form and send it, along with a check or money order for the total above,
payable to Silhouette Books, to: *In the U.S.:* 3010 Walden Avenue, P.O. Box 9077, Buffalo,
NY 14269-9077; *In Canada:* P.O. Box 636, Fort Erie, Ontario, L2A 5X3.

Name: _____

Address: _____ City: _____

State/Prov.: _____ Zip/Postal Code: _____

**New York residents remit applicable sales taxes.
  Canadian residents remit applicable GST and provincial taxes.

DMBACK

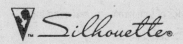